For seven months in 1989 a convicted murderer named Allan Legere was Canada's most-wanted man. Escaping from police custody May 3 in New Brunswick, Legere managed to elude hundreds of police officers equipped with helicopters, heat sensors, special night-vision eyewear, and tracking dogs.

In the meantime, a series of savage slayings rocked the province's picturesque Miramichi River region, throwing residents into a state of panic. With the arrival of winter, people hoped the snow and the cold would temper the killer's actions, force him to surrender or, at least, leave the province. However, the murder of a Roman Catholic priest in mid-November only served to heighten fears. The killer was still on the Miramichi and the tempo of his bloody deeds seemed to be increasing . . .

Terror: Murder and Panic in New Brunswick is the gut-wrenching story of a violence-plagued community living in a state of almost unrelieved anxiety. Written by two noted New Brunswick journalists, it's the definitive account of an event that gripped a province and captured the attention of a nation.

RICK MACLEAN AND ANDRÉ VENIOT

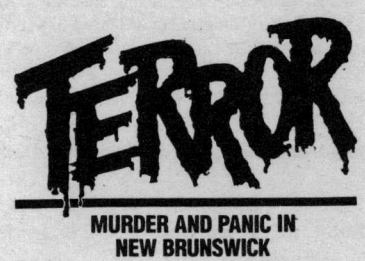

MURDER AND PANIC IN NEW BRUNSWICK

An M&S Paperback Original from
McClelland & Stewart Inc.
The Canadian Publishers

An M&S Paperback Original from McClelland & Stewart Inc.
First printing March 1990

Copyright © 1990 by Rick MacLean and André Veniot

All rights reserved. The use of any part of this publication reproduced, transmitted in any form or by any means, electronic, mechanical, photocopying, recording, or otherwise, or stored in a retrieval system, without the prior written consent of the publisher - or, in the case of photocopying or other reprographic copying, a licence from Canadian Reprographic Collective - is an infringement of the copyright law.

Canadian Cataloguing in Publication Data

MacLean, Rick, 1957-
Terror : murder and panic in New Brunswick

"An M&S paperback".
ISBN 0-7710-5592-7

1. Legere, Allan, 2. Murder - New Brunswick -
Miramichi Region. I. Veniot, André, 1950-
II. Title.

HV6535.C33M55 1990   364.1'523'0971521   C90-093355-0

Cover design by Tad Aronowicz
Front cover photograph: Canapress Photo Service/Andrew Vaughan
Front cover inset photograph: Canapress Photo Service/ RCMP
Back cover photographs (clockwise from left):
J.K.R. Walls; J.K.R. Walls; Canapress Photo Service/Andrew Vaughan

Typesetting by Tony Gordon Ltd.
Printed and bound in Canada

McClelland & Stewart Inc.
The Canadian Publishers
481 University Avenue
Toronto, Ontario
M5G 2E9

To our wives and families, with love. And to the people of the Miramichi, who didn't deserve what happened to them.

Contents

	Acknowledgements	ix
	Prologue	11
1.	"They Hurt Me Awful Bad"	13
2.	Months of Murder	23
3.	A People Shaped by a River	33
4.	A History of Sensational Murder Cases	41
5.	Guilty as Charged	49
6.	"The Devil in his Eyes"	65
7.	Escape	81
8.	Everyone Knew Annie	89
9.	Sudden Attacks	97
10.	Two Sisters Living a Quiet Life	101
11.	I've Got a Secret	109
12.	Safe in the House of God	123
13.	Guns under the Bed	133
14.	Locked Doors and Hidden Hammers	141
15.	"I Want a .357"	149
16.	"What He Done to My Son"	153
17.	The Love of the Chase	159
18.	Capture	167
19.	Centre-stage	179
	Epilogue	187

Acknowledgements

This book could not have been written without the help of many people, especially the nearly two dozen people who spoke with us, most on the condition of anonymity. That they still fear the past says much about what they went through.

Thanks to the staffs of the *Miramichi Leader* and the CBC News for New Brunswick, especially reporter Bonnie Sweeney of the *Leader* and cameraman Denis Butler, videotape editor Paul Landry, and reporter Bob Mersereau of the CBC.

Research done by *Times and Transcript*/Moncton librarian Nola O'Brien was a great help, as was some quick work by the staffs of the Old Manse Library in Newcastle and the Chatham town library.

Thanks as well to the *New Brunswick Telegraph Journal*, which produced some important material on Legere's early life, particularly for the work done by reporter Shaun Waters. Special thanks to the paper's editor, Howie Trainor.

Important work was also done by Canadian Press

reporters Stephen Thorne, Gerald Wesseen, and Chris Morris, and by photographer Andrew Vaughan.

Some key help was provided by David Cadogan, president of Cadogan Publishing Ltd. and publisher of the *Miramichi Leader*.

Photographer Ken Walls took many of the most important photos related to the story. Some are reprinted here with his permission.

Thanks to James Adams of McClelland & Stewart who first approached us with the idea for this book. And thanks as well to Fred and Pat Foran for their kindness and patience with two overwrought writers during three hectic weeks just before Christmas.

Any errors or omissions in this work are, of course, solely the responsibility of the authors.

PROLOGUE

Beginnings of Terror

The people of the Miramichi listened to their radios in terror on May 3, 1989, as they were told of the escape of convicted killer Allan Legere. Somehow he had slipped out of his shackles while in hospital that morning in Moncton, New Brunswick, then bolted past his guards, hijacked a car, and disappeared.

Legere's reputation as a break-and-enter artist with a violent temper had been well established in a life of crime that stretched back to his early teens. He was widely feared and regarded as extremely dangerous – a man capable of exploding at any time.

His escape marked the beginning of a seven-month reign of terror in the small towns and villages that make up the Miramichi region of northern New Brunswick, where Legere was born and grew up. Legere was finally captured on November 24, following a police effort that involved about a hundred officers and a cost of $1-million. He was caught after an all-night chase in which he hijacked a taxi and took the driver hostage, kidnapped an off-duty female RCMP officer, stole a tractor-trailer, and fled across half the province.

Three women and a Roman Catholic priest were murdered during the seven months Legere was at large. A fourth woman was recovering from a brutal attack that nearly killed her. Each attack seemed more vicious, more senseless, than the last. And the killer was increasing his pace. Four and a half months went by between the first and second killings; barely four weeks passed until the third. Police named Legere as their prime suspect, but they faced sharp criticisms for failing to swiftly catch whoever was responsible. The people of the region were living behind locked doors, each fearing he or she would be next.

The terror really began three years earlier, in the summer of 1986. It began at the home of an elderly couple running a store about 20 miles east of the town of Chatham.

ONE

"They Hurt Me Awful Bad"

ON JUNE 21, 1986, John and Mary Glendenning did what they always did Saturday nights between nine and nine-thirty. They closed their small general store, tidied up, then filled the pop machine before locking up and going home. It was a routine they'd followed since 1953, when they had opened the store in the rural area of Black River Bridge, about 20 miles east of Chatham.

Twenty minutes later they walked out the door and past the gas pumps, heading to their two-storey home just a few steps across the yard. The house was a large, square affair with an enclosed verandah on the front. Mary, then sixty-one, was known to keep it meticulously clean. Although in the country, the home and store were hardly isolated. Even though there were woods on the side of the house opposite the store, there were homes next to the store and across the road.

John walked through the pleasant summer night air to the garage to lock it up. He was a big man, balding, just under six feet tall, muscular with a barrel chest. He looked younger than his sixty-six years. Mary headed straight to the house and took a seat in the rocking chair in the kitchen. When her husband returned, she made a snack of jam, crackers, and cookies.

"We talked for a few minutes," Mary recalled, "and John called his brother Kenneth in Napan. He also made a call to a cousin in Bathurst. It would be after ten o'clock.

"I was sitting in my rocking chair finishing my tea. The dishes were still on the table. John was on the phone in the dining room.

"After the last call, he went in and turned on the television in the living room. I was still in the kitchen and going in to tell him something when I hear this desperate crash."

"What the hell is going on?" John yelled.

Three men had burst through the front door. One wore a tight-fitting nylon stocking that distorted his face. The second had a cap pulled over his eyes. The third, clearly older and heavier, hung back at first, staying by the door.

The one with the hat clubbed John, using a rock from the flower garden just outside.

"John was bleeding something awful hard," Mary recalled. "He kind of staggered back and sat on the rug by the couch."

"What do you want?" John cried. "I'll get it for you. You don't have to beat us around."

The man wearing the nylon came at Mary and shoved her into the kitchen. "He was very young, not over twenty. He pushed me in the chair, put my face down, and tied me there." He smashed her in the back on his way into the dining room, where he tore the phone out of the wall.

Mary's knots were poorly tied. She soon wriggled

free, all the while looking at the man standing in the doorway. He said nothing.

"When I got untied, I walked towards him. He picked up a rag and tried to gag me and tried to throw me in the closet in the front room. The younger guy, he took my clothes down, took my panties down. He put his hands all over me. John was still bleeding. John was on the floor with the other guy standing over him. The guy hit him. The third guy was still on the porch. John pleaded with them to leave us alone."

Glendenning said he would give his attackers whatever they wished. They ignored offers to take them over to the store. They knew about the safe upstairs and wanted the money inside.

"They never said much. I started to say something and the young lad said if I said anything, he would cut my ear off. The young guy spoke to the guy on the porch. I couldn't hear. The other guy asked where the safe was. John was trying to give him the combination. I think that was what John was trying to tell him."

She shouted that she would go up the stairs and open the safe if that's what they wanted. Her glasses were gone, however, and she could barely see.

"I started up the stairs and two guys came – the young guy and the one that was in the porch. The other young guy was still standing over John." It was the last time she saw her husband alive.

"I went right to the safe to see if I could open it. It was right in our bedroom. When I got hold of the dial I got severely hit on the head with something."

She turned to plead: "If you leave me alone, I'll open it for you." But that did no good.

"I just touched the dial when I got a more severe smack on the head. I never knew anything after that. I vaguely remember, though, I was in the toilet bowl." When she regained consciousness the three men were gone. The house was quiet. "It dawned on me, I had to call Margaret." Her daughter, Margaret Gibson, lived nearby.

Somehow, Mary managed to get to the upstairs phone. Luckily, it worked. The line for the downstairs phone had been cut but the three men obviously hadn't known the upstairs phone was a separate line. An operator took the call, knew something was horribly wrong, and patched the caller through to Rachelle Desroches at the RCMP's central dispatch in Moncton. Desroches had been with the force just fifteen months. She answered as she always did: "RCMP, GRC."

"Okay," the operator began. "I have this lady on the line. Someone broke into her house."

"Oh, they near killed us. Come quick," Mary groaned.

Desroches knew instantly it was bad, very bad. "They left. You just got home then?"

"No, I didn't. We've been here, they just about killed us. I bet they killed my husband, get somebody quick."

"Just stay on the line, just a moment."

"Yeah, we're both hurt. I don't know where John is. I'm upstairs, I can't get down."

Rachelle called RCMP officers in Newcastle, telling them they'd better get moving, fast. Mary was fading, she could feel it.

"Oh, I'm going to die."

"Just hang on. Did they hurt you?"

"Yeah."

"Did – What did they do to you?"

"They beat me around. They tried to rape me and everything."

Again, Rachelle talked to officers in Newcastle. She told Mary: "We got three cars going down to help you out."

Through her pain, Mary managed to give Rachelle her daughter's telephone number. Rachelle knew she had to keep Mary talking until help arrived.

"Oh, they hurt me awful bad."

"Oh, I know they did. And we're gonna get them for doing that to you, too."

Margaret was home reading in bed when the phone rang. Her husband, Aubrey, was asleep. As soon as they received the call, they jumped out of bed, into their truck, and and rushed to her parents' home.

Aubrey got to the house first. Margaret, who used a cane, followed as best she could.

"It was a mess. Everything was everywhere," Margaret said later. The verandah door was closed, but the main door was shattered, pieces of it everywhere.

The front hallway was a scene of horror. "We could see blood," Aubrey said, "or what appeared to be blood, on the floor and walls." Police later said there was blood dripping from the ceiling.

The Gibsons shouted to Mary and John. Hearing a faint sound from upstairs, Aubrey bolted up the steps, Margaret following as quickly as she could.

"Upstairs it was the same," Margaret said. "Everything was everywhere. There was glass all over the floor. The light had been broken out in the hall. The lighting was not all that good. I put on a light in the bedroom to the left, almost across from where she was sitting."

Aubrey found Mary. She was slumped in the doorway of the first bedroom on the right.

Margaret was stunned by what she saw. "If I hadn't known I was going to find my mother there, I wouldn't know it was her. She was badly bruised and swollen. She still had the phone in her hand. She was sitting on the floor."

Margaret gently took the phone out of her mother's hand. Desroches was still on the other end. Unable to speak, Margaret handed the phone to Aubrey.

"Listen," Desroches said, "we've got about six cars headed down there. Is your father okay?"

"We don't know anything yet," Aubrey said. "We can't find Mr. Glendenning." Assured that the police were on the way, he hung up.

Margaret tried to comfort her mother. "I pushed back her hair. It was wet. She colours her hair and I could smell the colouring on her. We got something and washed her face and Aubrey got her a drink of water."

Mary Glendenning was bleeding from the nose and mouth. She was trying to talk, but since she didn't have her dentures in, it was difficult to understand her.

There was something tied tightly around her neck. A scarf. It was tied so tightly Aubrey couldn't undo it. The best he could do was turn it around slightly to loosen it.

RCMP Const. Gilles Turgeon came through the door first, a twelve-gauge shotgun in his hands. Hearing voices, he ran up the stairs. He found Aubrey and Margaret with Mary. He cut the scarf from Mary's neck with a jackknife. Then he called to ensure the ambulance was on its way. He didn't hold out much hope. "She's on her way to dying," he thought to himself.

There was no immediate sign of John Glendenning, leading Turgeon to wonder if perhaps he might have been kidnapped. A few minutes later, however, Aubrey told him John was in the house. Dead.

He was upstairs, too, in the master bedroom, slumped on the floor behind the door, covered in blood. Even his socks were drenched in it. His hands had been tied with the electric cord from a digital clock, and his feet were tied with his braces. A light brown shirt was around his neck, tied at the back.

He had been brutally beaten. The mark of a shoe could be clearly seen on the right side of his face. A blood-stained rock the size of a grapefruit lay partly hidden beneath his head. His face was cut and scraped from the abuse. His nose was broken, as were a cheekbone and the right side of his jaw. But it was the shirt around the neck that had killed him. It had been so tightly tied that it had broken his Adam's apple.

Margaret Gibson went downstairs where a police officer gave her a sweater. She went outside and sat down on the step to wait for the ambulance. She looked down, spotted something on the ground. "They were store keys and a knife and rule my father always carries in his pocket."

Dr. Bill MacGillivray met Mary Glendenning at Hotel Dieu Hospital in Chatham. He'll always remember it.

"I couldn't believe a person could be as badly beaten and still be alive. The whole scalp area was bruised and swollen, everywhere I looked, every part of the body."

Her forehead had been broken by a severe blow. Both eyes were blackened and puffy. Her right eye was swollen shut, and when MacGillivray managed to pry it open to check it, he found a mass of blood.

Glendenning's nose was broken, and her right cheek badly scraped for about two inches. There was a three-inch slash below her left ear, a rectangular bruise nearly four inches long by her right ear. The left side of her neck and right shoulder were severely bruised. The shoulder was swollen. A blow to her left side had bruised her third rib. There were bruises, some as big as two inches in diameter, on her left hand.

Her right side was as bad. The hand was swollen. There was a bruise six inches long on her chest. The arm was swelling with seeping blood from an internal injury. One lung was damaged. Both legs were battered. Her assailants had also sexually assaulted her using a blunt object.

"I have never seen anything like it," MacGillivray said. "When I went home I couldn't sleep – and I've seen some pretty bad ones through the years."

Fred Ferguson was the crown prosecutor for the Miramichi. In law school, his classmates called him "Frantic Freddy" because he was always on the move.

He was good at his job. He'd put a lot of people behind bars in his fourteen years as a prosecutor.

Ferguson had been at a wedding that Saturday and had returned late to his Lower Newcastle home, late enough to see the full moon over the Miramichi River shining through his front door.

At 2:00 Sunday morning the RCMP called to tell him about the murder. He went to the Glendenning home later that morning. "It was an awful crime scene, full of mosquitoes and blood."

That evening he went to the RCMP detachment for a briefing on the Glendenning murder. En route, he drove past the McDonald's restaurant in Douglastown, between Chatham and Newcastle. Allan Legere, a well-known break-and-enter specialist, was pulling out of the parking lot, in his 240Z Datsun sports car.

"At the time no one had any idea who had committed the crime," Ferguson said. "I can remember our eyes met, an icy stare from him to me. I remember thinking, 'That's not a good look.'"

TWO

Months of Murder

THREE DAYS after the attack on the Glendennings, the police arrested three men. One was Allan Legere. A powerfully built man seen often at a local weight room, he was someone they knew well. At thirty-eight, he'd been in and out of jail since he was sixteen. His specialty was burglary, but he also had a history of violence. He was on parole, mandatory supervision.

Scott Curtis, twenty, and Todd Matchett, eighteen, had fled to Toronto, but soon gave themselves up and were taken back to face charges. Both had been involved in numerous petty crimes, mostly small thefts and break and enters.

Curtis was the bigger of the two, about six feet tall, his brown hair parted down the middle. He had been in trouble often as a teenager. At one point he left the Miramichi for a few years, working in Saint John in construction. But he moved back in early 1986 and quickly picked up where he had left off with Matchett.

Matchett was blond and about average in size. He was considered good-looking by teenage girls who knew him. The second of three children, he had two sisters. He came from a broken home. His father, Billy, ran a furniture store, but was widely suspected of operating on the shady side of the law, selling stolen goods. His wife, Dorothy, eventually left him and did her best to keep the family going on her own, working for a time at a local clothing store. Todd had a bad temper and was known for throwing tantrums when he was younger.

Police found the Glendennings' safe quickly. It was in the woods off the Kelly Road on the south end of Chatham. The money was gone, thousands of dollars of it. Most was never recovered.

From the start, the case captured the attention of the people of the Miramichi. Police tried to keep a lid on, but people soon knew that Matchett and Curtis had taken off to Saint John in a red car and from there headed to Toronto.

Curtis and Matchett were charged in Newcastle court on Monday, July 7, with murder and attempted murder. Legere was charged the next day. Both court appearances were a sensation, especially Legere's. Hundreds waited outside to catch a glimpse of him.

"You should be hanged," people shouted as he walked up the stone steps into the Newcastle courthouse, an imposing two-storey stone building on the busiest corner in town.

Security inside was tight. The second-floor courtroom was packed. The crowd spilled into the hallway and down the stairs. People in the balcony leaned forward, straining to see Legere. The judge, Drew Stymiest, told them to sit down.

The hearing went quickly. Legere's second court date was set for the following week. The accused stood up, then stopped to stare at the crowd in the balcony.

Outside, police were having a tough time preventing

drivers eager to see Legere from slamming into each other as they forgot to stop at traffic lights. A parking lot across the street – normally less than half full – was jammed with cars and people. Parked cars and a large crowd blocked the entrance to a service station opposite the courthouse.

The courthouse is built on a hill overlooking the town. A small lawn in front ends abruptly at a stone retaining wall that drops about three feet to the sidewalk. People jammed onto that narrow bit of sidewalk too, waiting. Police had to force a path through the throng before escorting Legere to a car waiting at the bottom of the courthouse steps.

The three men appeared the next Monday to set the date for a preliminary hearing. It was a cold windy day, and despite a driving rain a crowd turned out – as it would for every court appearance. The preliminary hearing, held to see if there was enough evidence for a trial, was set for September 9 in Newcastle. Legere was sent to the maximum security prison in Dorchester, a village near Moncton, about ninety miles away. Matchett and Curtis were held in jail cells in Moncton.

Tensions in the community eased somewhat. People had been shocked by the brutality of the attack on the Glendennings and were relieved by the arrests. Still, some elderly people feared they might be next.

Local doctor Jerry Wilson could see what the fear was doing to some of his patients, particularly one woman. "She wasn't my patient. I was covering for another doctor. Her history showed an abnormal heartbeat. It had been skipping, but had gotten much worse after the murder. I questioned her on it, although she lived in Nelson and the murder happened miles away. She told me yes, she blamed it for her condition. She was the very best as long as family was around, but just as soon as they left, her heart started beating irregular and skipping again. She told me that when she was alone, all she could think about was the Glendenning murder."

The peace following the arrests proved short-lived. The Glendenning murder was to be but a prelude to a series of other killings that summer and fall on the Miramichi.

The killing began again on August 12. At six-thirty that Tuesday morning family members, after an all-night search, found two young girls who had been missing since overnight. Tara Prokosh, thirteen, was dead. Her fourteen-year-old friend, Gina Guitard, was barely alive. They had been sexually assaulted, stabbed, and left for dead next to a hunting camp built beside the Bartibogue River, about twelve miles north of Chatham. The camp, a small wooden building, was at the end of a dirt road, minutes from Tara's home in the rural community of Russellville. Tara and Gina had cycled down the road to the river sometime after seven-thirty Monday night. It was Gina's parents who found the girls.

One police officer said it was a sight he would never forget, Tara's body lying next to the camp, the girls' bicycles leaning against the building. He vowed he would catch the person who could do such a thing, no matter how long it took.

A couple of hours after the girls were found, *Miramichi Leader* reporter Bonnie Sweeney worked her way through the woods to take photos of the camp. She didn't know until her film was developed in the afternoon that one of the photos showed a figure draped in a blanket. Staff gathered to decide what to do. The *Leader*, a twice-weekly with sales of about nine thousand each edition, had a reputation for breaking stories and being hard-hitting, but this was different. A deadline looming, the staff decided to run the photo.

The attack, coming so soon after the Glendenning killing and involving two young girls, stunned the region. Parents stopped letting their children go out alone after dark. They looked for ways to street-proof their kids.

"Perhaps we've been taking things too lightly," crime prevention officer Lawrence Burns of the Newcastle police told a reporter. "We tend to think of these things happening in bigger cities. It's happened right here."

He described precautions taken by his son and daughter-in-law living in the village of Douglastown, next to Newcastle. They refused to let their children out of their sight. "I've talked to a number of people in that area," Burns said. "They're all scared. That fellow is still loose, he hasn't been caught yet. And even if he's not, who's to say there's not another person like him out there who could do the same thing?"

Burns's job often took him to schools to talk about safety. "We tell them to screech and yell, which may scare off their attacker. But," he conceded, "in a secluded area such as where this murder happened, it's doubtful this would be very good."

Anger and fear prompted a call for tougher penalties for convicted killers.

"Everyone is talking about bringing back the death penalty," said Jack Bell, then Chatham's deputy police chief. "That's the first thing that comes to mind when something like this happens. And this always brings up the subject of letting criminals out on parole. Several times I've heard the comment that it's probably someone who's on mandatory supervision."

Politicians got involved.

"The hands of the police are tied in a lot of cases," Newcastle Mayor John McKay suggested. "We have a situation where the judicial system has to bear some responsibility. There's no excuse for people who have already committed crimes to be allowed to carry out another act."

The case drew national attention. Toronto was just recovering from the killing of Alison Parrott, thirteen, found beaten to death in a wooded area of the city. The *Toronto Sun* sent reporter B.J. Del Conte down to cover the story. He found young people frightened. "I don't feel any safer because I'm a guy," said Doug Briggs, sixteen. "You can't have that attitude. I like to go for walks in the woods, but I won't go by myself anymore. Even the little kids understand that."

Nine days after the Prokosh-Guitard incident, Newcastle town council approved a $1,000 reward for information leading to the arrest and conviction of the killer. A reward fund was set up at a local bank by two men from nearby Tracadie.

That Friday the weekend edition of the *Miramichi Leader* printed the results of a write-in poll on capital punishment. More than a hundred people had responded. All but a few favoured bringing back the noose. Their comments filled four pages. "Society must be protected against certain types of criminals, i.e. murderers. Not only a deterrent is capital punishment, but also a guarantee that a murderer will never kill anyone else," Norman Savage of Douglastown wrote on his ballot.

The police were flooded with tips, especially after they released a composite sketch of the man involved in the attack. First there were a hundred calls, then five hundred. By mid-September the figure topped nine hundred. One tip named a slightly built twenty-two-year-old millworker with blondish hair and big hands. It was a good tip, better than most. But when police had to decide which calls to check first and which to put on hold, they held off following up on that tip. It's a decision police dread. This time, they were wrong. It may have cost a second teenager her life.

Against that backdrop of fear, the Glendenning case resumed. On September 9, the courtroom filled for the preliminary hearing. Crowds waited outside to see who came and went. The downstairs of the courtroom was packed, but not with spectators. Only reporters, witnesses, and family members were allowed in. There was no room left after that. Court officials turned away about a dozen people who tried to get in. Some managed to squeeze into the balcony, which was open to the public.

The next day, the court ordered Legere, Matchett, and Curtis to stand trial. They chose to be tried by a judge and jury. A trial date was to be determined later.

On Monday, September 22, the body of nineteen-year-old single mother Theresa MacLaughlin was found in a gravel pit near her home in the village of Neguac, a short drive north of where Tara Prokosh had been murdered. The killer had beaten MacLaughlin to death with a blunt object.

MacLaughlin had spent September 21 at home with her adoptive parents, Johnny, seventy-eight, and May, seventy-two. She had failed a couple of courses that spring, but was returning to high school to get the credits she needed to graduate. She wanted to take a postsecondary course of some kind so she could support herself and her eight-month-old son, Daniel Scott.

At nine that evening, MacLaughlin decided to go to the nearby A&M Superette. Her son was asleep for the night. John MacLaughlin drove his daughter to the store and dropped her off. He never saw her alive again.

The community barely had time to react before police arrested Kenneth Esson, a millworker from Nelson-Miramichi, and charged him with two counts of murder and one count of attempted murder. Esson, it turned out, bore such a close resemblance to a police sketch of the suspected killer that his fellow employees joked with him about it. Esson had attempted to downplay the resemblance by perming his hair.

His first court appearance occurred in a circus-like atmosphere. It was at 4:30 P.M. on September 25. There's a large school complex just up the street from the Newcastle courthouse, and the sidewalks were jammed with students pushing and shoving, trying to see the man charged with killing one of their classmates. Students hung out the windows of passing school buses, hoping to see the accused.

The eight policemen escorting Esson into the courthouse dwarfed him, who, at five foot six, looked almost frail.

The shouting began. "Electrocute him! Hang him by his toes from the courthouse! Why bring him here? Why not just slaughter him and get it over with?"

The ordeal seemed over, for the community as a whole, and for one family in particular. Two months after Esson was charged, Mervyn and Jane Houck of Russellville told the *Miramichi Leader* of their ordeals. Rumours had pointed a finger at their son, Michael, saying he was the killer. He resembled the sketch police were circulating, and nasty talk began to spread. One day, Mervyn was in a grocery store and heard two women talking. "They were there standing talking about my son, and there were others standing around who heard it."

While Esson was in Saint John for psychiatric observation yet another murder occurred. On the morning of October 14, the body of Patrick Murphy, thirty-nine, of Chatham, was found by the river near downtown. He had been stabbed to death.

The killings and court dates seemed to blur together. Esson was ordered to stand trial, which he did the next spring. He pleaded guilty and was sentenced to life with no chance of parole for twenty-five years. Earl Lewis, forty-two, of Chatham, was charged with murdering Murphy. He was out of prison after serving time for an earlier killing. He claimed self-defence, saying Murphy had attacked him when they were both drinking down by the river. Lewis was later convicted and jailed.

All the while, the Glendenning case was slowly working its way to trial, but not without a final twist thrown in. On November 7, Legere was stabbed while in prison in Dorchester. It was a bad wound – the homemade knife was rammed a full six inches into his back, narrowly missing his heart. Legere was taken to hospital with a punctured lung. Scott Curtis was charged with assault, but the case didn't make it to court.

A few days after the attack, the murder trial date was set – Tuesday, January 6.

On December 17, Legere tried to have his case moved out of the Miramichi, saying he could not get a fair trial there. Lawyers for Matchett and Curtis also tried that day to have their cases heard separately from

Legere's. Court of Queen's Bench Judge Paul Godin turned them all down.

The sparring was over. A trial that would capture the attention of the people of the Miramichi like none before it was set to begin.

THREE

A People Shaped by a River

It's now I will take up my pen
Those verses for to write.
Concerning of this river
I mean for to recite.
For all through nature's splendor
There's none that I can see
Like the rolling tide that flows 'longside
The banks of the Murrymashee.

Its little trout and salmon
Are playing night and day,
The feathered throng assemble
Their beauty to display.
And sportsmen there do gather
And all delight to see
The rolling tide that flows 'longside
The banks of the Murrymashee.

If I had gold and silver
Brought from some foreign place,
And r'yal robes put on me
And a crown set o'er my face,

I would yield it all with pleasure,
But sooner would I be
Where the rolling tide it flows 'longside
The banks of the *Murrymashee*.

("The Banks of the Miramichi." Lyrics by Patrick Hurley.
Songs of the Miramichi, ed. Louise Manny and
James Reginald Wilson, 1968)

IT'S A beautiful place, ideal for fishermen and people who love hunting and the woods. It looks like anything but a home for killers. And that's why people living on the Miramichi are so angry when they read derogatory news reports about their area. It's a place where neighbours know each other and do what they can to help.

The Miramichi is a collection of small towns, villages, and rural communities stretching for about 180 miles along the Miramichi River and its tributaries. Estimates vary, but about 50,000 live along the river system that stretches from the tiny English-speaking lumbering community of Boiestown in the middle of New Brunswick, past Newcastle and nearby Chatham about sixty miles downstream, then out to Miramichi Bay and such French-speaking fishing villages as Neguac and Escuminac near the mouth of the river.

The river is the key. It's a sight capable of taking away the breath of any visitor – especially in the fall when the birch, maple, and poplar turn the riverbanks into corridors of reds, oranges, and yellows. The river, and those trees, have shaped the local economy and people from the beginning.

The Miramichi – believed to be a variation on an Indian word meaning "land of the Micmacs" – had been home to the Micmac tribe for thousands of years. Trees drew white men to the area. The river enabled them to get the trees to markets first in Europe and later in the United States. The first white settler thought to have landed in the area was Nicolas Denys around 1650. He discovered a river teeming with fish, particularly salmon, and ringed by huge stands of ramrod-straight pine.

English settlement of the Miramichi dates from the arrival of William Davidson in the 1760s. Davidson and his friend, John Cort, were granted land in exchange for a promise to settle it. Indian raids and fear of American attack during the Revolutionary War made for tough going, but the settlement gradually took hold and grew.

Early on, the Miramichi developed a reputation for intense internal rivalries on the one hand and a sense of separation from the rest of what would later become New Brunswick on the other. Miles of woods separated the region from such places as Fredericton to the south and Moncton to the east. The river separated the two largest towns in the area, Newcastle on the north and Chatham on the south.

The towns have been rivals since they were established. They are nearly identical in size – Chatham's population in 1988 was 6,219, Newcastle had 5,804 residents – and just over six miles apart. But working together has been difficult. In the election of 1843, there were pitched battles in the streets as leaders and followers from both sides fought for supremacy.

The disagreements continue to this day, though they tend to be more peaceful. A recent row erupted over a decision by the president of a provincial high school hockey league to discipline the Newcastle team for rowdy behaviour. The president happened to be from Chatham. Some Newcastle people thought that affected his decision. By the time the fight was over, Newcastle had decided to switch to another league.

One thing the two towns and surrounding communities agree on is politics. The area's traditionally Liberal sentiments date back to Fathers of Confederation John Mercer Johnson and Peter Mitchell. A flirtation with the Conservatives in 1984 ended four years later when the riding bucked the national trend and returned to voting Liberal.

Today the area is best known politically for the member of the provincial legislature representing Chatham, Premier Frank McKenna. It is also the home of the leader of the newly formed Confederation of Regions party, Arch Pafford. The party, although founded in western Canada, has found some success in New Brunswick by playing on English fears of the large francophone population in the province. Those tensions have always been a part of the fabric of the Miramichi, an area with a number of Acadian villages along its shoreline. Anglophones fear the rise of bilingualism and say the growing demand for people capable of speaking both languages, especially in the highly prized and well-paying government jobs, threatens their chances to earn a living. Pafford placed third in the 1987 provincial election, trailing the Liberals and Conservatives, but ahead of the New Democrats.

Like so much of the Maritimes, the Miramichi has known its share of tough times. Until a few years ago, the unemployment rate in the area was about 50 percent. It's not a new story.

Joseph Cunard moved to the Miramichi in 1821 to start a shipbuilding business. A big man, six feet tall and weighing over two hundred pounds, he set out to build a big business. By 1839, he owned two shipyards in Chatham and had about five hundred men turning out a ship every two weeks. Eight years later, hurt by a depression and the arrival of the steamship, he was broke. Hundreds of angry unemployed workers took to the streets yelling "Shoot Cunard!" Joseph survived and later left for good, moving to England. His family there eventually paid his debts. His brother, Samuel, would lead the family to prominence as the creator of the famous Cunard international shipping line.

Perhaps the most famous businessman to come out of the Miramichi was Max Aitken, later known as Lord Beaverbrook. Although born in Maple, Ontario, in 1879, he grew up in Newcastle. He quickly rose from being a lawyer in Chatham to a newspaper magnate in England. He was an aide to Churchill during the Second World War, helping guide aircraft production.

The Miramichi stays in the blood of those who live there, and Beaverbrook is a good example. As a rich British lord, he remembered Newcastle, providing money for public buildings. He also rebuilt the town square, adding lights and a gazebo. Today, his ashes are buried there, under an imposing statue of himself that faces the town hall bearing his name.

Beaverbrook left to make his fortune, but many over the years have stayed, braving the tough times, waiting for a change of luck. One came in 1985, when the Montreal-based company Repap – paper spelled backwards – bought the pulp mill. The mill in Newcastle dominates the skyline and the economy. It has changed hands often since 1949, when it was built, and seemed certain to close eventually until Repap stepped in and invested nearly a billion dollars. Today, the mill produces coated paper for magazines and employs about three thousand. The money spent to get it going has touched off a boom.

A military base in Chatham, a mine north of Newcastle, and a maximum-security prison in the small community of Renous, about eighteen miles south of Newcastle, are also important to the local economy, yet, as in past centuries, the river and the forests are what keep the region going.

Locals will tell you in no uncertain terms that the river is the world's finest for Atlantic salmon, a major draw for sports fishermen from around the world. A keen fisherman of Miramichi waters for years was Ted Williams, the former Boston Red Sox player and the last man in the major leagues to bat .400.

There are concerns about the health of the river. A Domtar wood-treatment plant operated in Newcastle for years, treating such wood products as hydro poles with chemicals to prevent rotting. Documents uncovered in the late 1980s showed that both the company and the provincial government knew there were serious problems with leaks from the plant, yet they did nothing. Only a change in governments and months of public pressure forced the company to admit that it was responsible and pushed the government into ordering a cleanup. That incident seems to have galvanized people in the area. The Repap mill now faces pressure to clean up its act, something it says it is doing. Municipalities in the area are looking into setting up a regional dump after residents near the Chatham dump blocked it to protest the poor way it was being run. Newcastle continues to wrestle with concerns about its water. Tests in 1988 and 1989 detected cancer-causing chemicals in the water, and people were forced to drink water trucked in from outside. There is now a debate about the quality of the tests, and the town continued to supply containers of drinking water while new studies were done in early 1990.

Even the music of the region tells of the rivers and woods. The annual Miramichi Folksong Festival was started in 1957 because of the interest of Louise Manny, who went around the region collecting folksongs about the lumberjacks and the lives of the people along the river. Her work helped preserve that tradition of history remembered in song. It also prompted a move to name a "mountain" after her – Manny Mountain – about forty-five miles northeast of Newcastle.

And when people talk about the Miramichi in the 1980s, they like to talk about the success of things like the Irish festival, which draws thousands from across Canada and the States each year.

They don't like talking about murder.

FOUR

A History of Sensational Murder Cases

PEOPLE DISLIKE talking about it, but the Miramichi is no stranger to sensational murders and murder trials.

Legend has it that long ago a nun was murdered by pirates at a cove near Newcastle. Her head was sawed off and her body buried along with the pirates' treasure. There are people who say she can be seen there yet, wandering the cove, looking for her head.

A folksong written by Michael Whelan, "the Poet of the Renous" (1857-1938), preserves the memory of a curly-haired camp cook who allegedly was murdered in the dark, deep woods of central New Brunswick. The shrieking ghost of the cook came to be known as the Dungarvon Whooper (named after the Dungarvon River, a tributary of the Renous River).

The cook's "unearthly whoops and screams and yells" were silenced years later when a Catholic priest, Edward Murdoch, performed the rite of exorcism. To this day, however, people continue to swear that the wails of the Whooper can still be heard occasionally. A train named after the noisy ghost ran between Newcastle and Fredericton until 1936.

Murders and murder cases of the more modern variety dot the area's history too. One of the strangest stories came to be known as the Great Bumblebee Case. It involved Joe Mercure, who, at age sixty-two, was convicted of killing ninety-one-year-old Patrick Martin during a robbery.

Mercure grew up on the Miramichi. His mother died when he was seven, and he quit school to help out at home. It was a tough time to find work. It was made even tougher in the 1930s when the depression kicked a hole in what little prosperity people enjoyed.

Mercure eventually moved out on his own, working in the woods around the small community of Craigville, south of Newcastle. He married at age fifteen and fathered sixteen children. He was known as a difficult man to deal with when he'd had a drink, and he loved to drink. By the 1940s, his wife had left him.

He tried his luck working at farms in Maine for a time, making anywhere from fifty cents to a dollar a day. There was even a stint in Sept-Iles, Quebec, working on the boats there. But the Miramichi was his home, and he headed back.

That was a mistake. One day in 1963, police came to pick him up. He was suspected of killing Martin, who was found in the kitchen of his Douglasfield home, near the area where Mercure grew up. Martin had been hit over the head and his body burned by someone using newspapers to start the fire. An RCMP investigation pointed the finger at Mercure, so police searched his home. There, in the wood stove, they found Martin's bank book and a wallet containing a dollar bill.

The police shipped their find off to the crime lab for

a closer look, and that's when what had been a rather ordinary case took an extraordinary turn. Researchers using microscopes found two things – a tiny fleck of blood on the dollar bill, and stuck to that blood a speck of something that looked like a piece of branch. The bill was shipped to Ottawa, where a visiting scientist from the United States determined that the branch was, in fact, the hair from the leg of a bumblebee common to the part of New Brunswick where Martin had lived.

Police returned to Martin's home to thoroughly search it, hoping to find the rest of the bee. An officer opened a roll-top desk. Bits of the bee were there. More searching uncovered additional fragments in the pocket of a jacket Martin had owned.

It took two trials to convict Mercure: the first ended in a hung jury; at the second, he was sentenced to hang, but his penalty was later commuted to life in prison.

"Old Joe" Mercure died in November 1986, at age eighty-six. Just three years earlier, he had made headlines when he became the oldest prisoner in a Canadian prison. He died – in a nursing home where he was sent because of illness – protesting his innocence.

Another murder story that continues to live on in the minds of the people of the Miramichi began on March 23, 1974. That evening, Beatrice Mary Redmond walked down the steps of the Nativity of the Blessed Virgin Mary Roman Catholic Church in Chatham Head after attending mass. The fifty-six-year-old got into her car and headed for home, about half a mile away. She stopped at Henderson's, the neighbourhood service station and grocery store, to pick up a few items. She left the store around a quarter to eight, going to her home just around the corner. Her daughter was supposed to call that evening from Ottawa, and Redmond wanted to make certain she was there when the phone rang. She never made it.

Redmond's body was found face down in the little porch leading to her apartment on the second floor of a two-storey building near the river. She had been stabbed nearly eighty times. There was no sign of blood, prompting speculation she was killed elsewhere, then dragged or carried to her home. The tam she was wearing when she died, a three-quarter-length leather coat, and her purse were gone.

Her mother, Mrs. Frank McMahon, lived with her in the apartment and was home that night, but heard nothing. Redmond's husband was away visiting relatives. Mrs. Frank McLaughlin and her two children, David and Nancy, lived downstairs. David was out that night. Nancy had been at church. Their mother was home all night, yet she heard nothing either.

Redmond's car was spotted in her yard at eight o'clock. The tam, purse, and coat were never found. The knife used to kill her was never found either.

More than a hundred investigators tried cracking the case over the years, and every time the smallest bit of new information turned up officers were sent to check it. There was even an investigation carried out overseas because ships were docked at the time in Newcastle, a five-minute walk across the Morrissy Bridge that links the two communities. The results were always the same – nothing.

In September 1987, Crime Stoppers, an independent organization that encourages anonymous tips to a special phone line, tried one more time. Crime Stoppers produces television re-enactments of crimes, in the hope that someone who sees them will call with new information. The murder of Redmond was filmed incorporating what few facts the police knew. A house similar to Redmond's had to be used because hers had been torn down. The re-enactment produced three tips, but nothing concrete.

In March 1988, RCMP officer Kevin Mole approached the *Miramichi Leader* about running a story on the efforts to solve the murder. The article appeared on the front page with the headline "Chasing a killer – 14 years later." This effort also failed. The case remains unsolved.

One of the most compelling murder episodes in the history of the Miramichi involved a noted Canadian boxer. On the evening of May 20, 1977, Yvon Durelle stepped out of his Baie Ste. Anne bar. He had a gun. What happened next catapulted him into the legal limelight. It also helped make the reputation of an up-and-coming lawyer from Chatham, the man who ten years later would become premier of New Brunswick – Frank McKenna.

Durelle was already a famous man. In 1958, at the age of twenty-eight, he knocked down light-heavyweight world champion Archie Moore twice in the first round of a title fight. A long count and the bell saved the middle-aged Moore, who went on to win the fight. Still, Durelle's place in history was assured.

After his fighting career ended, Durelle bounced from job to job, finding financial success only in the mid-1970s, when he opened The Fisherman's Club. Thanks to the bar's success, Durelle was able to pay off old debts. He seemed ready to settle into a life of some prosperity in his home area. The only problem was Albin Poirier.

Poirier had a reputation for being unstable. In 1975 a police officer had gone to his trailer and found him lying on the floor, his stomach slashed open in an apparent suicide attempt, parts of his organs spilling out. Poirier was yelling, "You won't tap my phone! You won't open my mail!"

Two years later, Poirier was causing problems at Durelle's club. He would sit at tables where he wasn't wanted and be such a nuisance that Durelle was forced to evict him. And it was getting worse. That May, he had been thrown out four times in one week, once for splashing beer in a man's face, another time for slugging someone for no reason.

Durelle called the Newcastle RCMP on the afternoon of May 20 to complain, but was told that since it was Friday, he'd have to wait until Monday to get a court order banning Poirier from the club.

At nine o'clock that evening Poirier telephoned Durelle. "Yvon, you've got three days to get out of Baie Ste. Anne," he snarled. A few minutes later he called back. The deadline had changed to two hours.

Sometime after midnight Poirier showed up at the club and tried to get in. Durelle walked to the door to meet him, picking up a .38 pistol on his way.

"Albin," Durelle said, "we've been friends a long time. I lend you money. I buy you drinks. I'm like a father to you. Why do you treat me like this?"

"Times have changed, Yvon," Poirier growled.

Durelle took Poirier to his car. Poirier got in, started it, then backed up, slamming into a parked vehicle. Then he shot forward, trying to run Durelle down.

Although not known for being quick on his feet even when he was boxing, Durelle stumbled out of the way.

Poirier tried again, missed and rammed a second car. Durelle ran towards him. The car advanced again and Durelle started shooting. Poirier's car veered right at the first shot and crashed into a third car. Durelle ran up to Poirier's car and fired through the window four times.

Poirier died of five gunshot wounds, one to the head and four to the chest. Durelle was arrested. The trial that began on September 12 was a national sensation.

There was some damning testimony early on. Witness Robert Robichaud said Durelle came back into the club after the shooting joking about what he had done. "He said, 'I got him good the first time. I shot him in the face. It was just like shooting beer bottles or a duck. Poirier's jacket wasn't too thick. The bullets went through real easy.'"

But Chatham police chief Dan Allen told of seeing a different Durelle the morning after the shooting. Durelle's face was pressed against the bars as he sobbed, "I'm no murderer. Chief, I can't take it. I'm better off dead."

Frank McKenna and co-counsel Denis Lordon decided on the bold strategy of putting Durelle on the stand. It was a risky move for Durelle was unpredictable and could easily hurt his own case. He described with pride the violence of his boxing days: "I loved to hit guys over the head. I used to look at their faces when I knocked them down. Jeez, they had a funny expression. I seen niggers turn white and whites turn black."

In another case, such talk might have been damning, but not here.

Author Raymond Fraser covered the trial for the

Miramichi Press. In his book about Durelle, *The Fighting Fisherman*, Fraser noted that the ex-boxer left people with the clear impression that he was "a simple, befuddled, and basically harmless man who had been driven to an extreme."

Attempts by the Crown prosecutor to capitalize on his chances failed. At one point, Durelle turned the tables on him. "Poirier tried to run me down," he said. "I was scared for my life. If someone tried to run you down, sir, wouldn't you be scared?"

Yes, the prosecutor said, he would be.

"Well, so was I."

By the time the judge was ready to turn the case over to the jury it seemed like a foregone conclusion. Mr. Justice Ronald Stevenson said, "The defence of self-defence fails only if the Crown has proved beyond a reasonable doubt that the accused was not in fear of his life." The jury returned in ninety minutes. The verdict was not guilty.

FIVE

Guilty as Charged

THURSDAY, January 8, 1987. The trial of Allan Legere, Todd Matchett, and Scott Curtis was into its third day before a jury of eleven men and one woman. The trial was scheduled to last three weeks and it was starting slowly, as the Crown waded through technical evidence.

Matchett and Curtis appeared loose and relaxed. Matchett returned to the courthouse after lunch one day and made some dancing motions with his shackled feet. It was a shuffle, as if he was pretending the leg irons forced him to walk that way. He smiled to a sister and talked to her and others in his family. Inside the courtroom Curtis was smoking. "They won't let *me* smoke over here," Matchett joked when he entered. A guard told Curtis to put out the cigarette. It all seemed so normal.

Then Matchett's lawyer got up to announce that his client was pleading guilty. Matchett looked calm as he told Mr. Justice Paul Godin of the Court of Queen's Bench that he understood he was facing a life sentence with no chance of parole for at least ten years.

His thoughts were his own that day. But nearly three weeks later when he returned to hear his sentence – life without parole for sixteen years – he managed to slip a letter to a CBC TV reporter.

Neatly printed in pencil, but full of misspellings, it read: "I Todd Matchett, was involved in an arm robbery at the home of Mr. and Mrss'es Glendenings. But I'm truly telling the truth when I say that I wasn't planing on beating or hurting anyone of the Glendening's. Although Mr. Glendening met his death and Mrs. Glendening got a very bad beating, I just want it known that I Todd Matchett had nothing to do with the beatings of either of the Glendenings. What I was told was that the safe was just to be removed. I was also told to go in and ties the people, the Glendenings that is go up and take the safe and just leave, and that's just what I wanted to, but as you can see it just didn't work out that way did it? Although when I left the house I thought that both of the Glendening's were *alive*. I just went to do a robbery and I didn't do anything to hurt anybody, and now it turn's out that I'm getting charged for a murder and an attempted murder. I really never thought that if you didn't have anything to do with the beating, that you, your self couldn't be charged with the actual murder even if I didn't have any part in the beating death of Mr. Glendening. Also, I Todd William Matchett, will not testify against anyone because if I'm going down for a murder that I didn't comite, because I'd just rather do my time and get out of the pen as soon as possible."

The letter was signed by Matchett. There were also notes crammed into a small space at the top of the page. One read, "It just so happened that I was accompanyed with a (nut), better known as a (sicko)." The second note said, "The only way that the truth is going to come out on what really happened on the night of June 21/86 is in the book I'm writting on my life."

A second sheet contained a half page of writing, also in pencil: "Well as you can see Allan Legere really did a good job on putting everything on use me and Scott that is and taking everything off himself. everyone heard what Allan said and believed it but no one heard what really happened and me and Scott will shed alot of light on what really happened that night, and everybody will see what really took place that night. Allan put all the blame on us because of what happened to him while he was awaiting trail, when he got stabed, and he thinks that Scott was involved in it."

The drama continued through the afternoon. Curtis pleaded guilty as well, calmly admitting his role in the death of John Glendenning.

Only Legere was left. People speculated that he might plead guilty and the trial could be over soon. Mary Glendenning and her daughter, Margaret Gibson, were due to testify next. No one knew how Mary would bear up in the witness box. If Legere pleaded guilty, she wouldn't have to testify; it would be a small bit of justice.

There was no guilty plea that day, however. Nor the next. In fact, not ever. Years later, Legere would continue to maintain his innocence, continue to say that he – like Donald Marshall, the Nova Scotia Indian wrongfully convicted of murder and jailed for eleven years – was a victim of a miscarriage of justice.

Called to the witness stand, Margaret Gibson described finding her mother in what was left of her home. Her parents owned a safe and kept it upstairs in their bedroom, she said. Her father always kept a fair amount of cash on him – between $300 and $500. Legere's lawyer, David Hughes, regarded as one of the top criminal lawyers in the province, asked Gibson who might know about the safe and if she was ever concerned about her parents keeping money in the house. She knew of no one who had heard about the safe. Yes, she was worried about her parents with the money there, "but that's the way they were."

Speaking quietly, and struggling to hold back tears, Mary Glendenning described the attack. She told of her futile attempts to give the killers what they wanted and of the call to her daughter.

There had been a warning of sorts prior to the attack, she revealed. About eight days earlier, on a Friday night, a car had stopped in their yard and backed up to the garage. "I told John there was a reddish colour car backed up . . . I looked out the window and saw it. By the time I called John, it had moved, and he just saw it going through the laneway."

Later that same night she had heard a car pull up to the front door, but by the time they got out of bed to look, it was heading slowly away from the house. The next day she noticed the downstairs phone wasn't working. A repairman came to fix it. "He asked me if I had cut the wires . . . to get him down there. He was joking, but the wires looked as if they had been cut."

Asked about her health since the attack, Mary said she still couldn't sleep with the back of her head on a pillow because of a blow she had received during the attack.

There was no cross-examination.

The trial riveted the public. The *Miramichi Leader* provided blanket coverage of the case. Reporter Bonnie Sweeney, using her ability to take shorthand, provided newspaper page after newspaper page of coverage. The twice-weekly was delaying publication by a couple of hours each Tuesday and Thursday so it could include the latest testimony. Lineups of people waited for its arrival in stores. One evening in Newcastle an estimated 125 persons anticipated the paper's arrival at a service station known to be among the first stops on the delivery route.

As the second week of the trial began, twenty-one-year-old Donald Langan, a long-time associate of Matchett with a record of break and enters, took the stand. The robbery was Legere's idea, he said. Legere knew about the safe and he recruited the others to help him steal from it.

The planning had started the weekend before the attack. Matchett and Langan ran into Legere twice; each time he said there was easy money to be had at the Glendenning home – at least $15,000. He was willing to take them there, but they had to go in and get the safe. They drove by the house to check it out, recruiting Scott Curtis to help them. On June 18 they met in Chatham, ready to go after the safe.

"Allan was driving," Langan recalled. "Todd was in the front. Me and Scott laid down in the back. We went by a little garage and Scott put on coveralls. Todd put on a jacket. Scott put on a pair of gloves, and I put on a pair of gloves. Scott had a nylon on. Todd had a nylon on. Todd gave me one, but it didn't fit. Todd had a sawed-off sixteen-gauge shotgun. Scott, I'm pretty sure, he had a knife. When Legere dropped us off he just went up the road on the Baie Ste. Anne side and parked, maybe by the rec centre or hall."

They were about two or three hundred feet from the house. They worked their way to some small brush, then they spotted a light in an upstairs bedroom. Too risky, they decided, and turned back, dumping clothing and a gun along the way.

"We were all scared of Allan because we knew he wanted it done. Todd did the talking. He said he didn't feel right about it, there was a light on, probably someone was home, and he didn't want to go through with it."

Legere was angry and shouted at them all the way back to Chatham. "He said it should be done, there was fifteen grand in it."

The next time he saw Legere, Langan said, was June 22, the day after the killing. Legere showed up at the garage where Langan worked. He said nothing, just drove up and pointed his index finger at Langan, moving his thumb up and down as if it were the hammer of a pistol. Langan took it as a threat: he would be killed if he said anything.

On January 15, RCMP Sgt. Mason Johnston took the stand. His testimony was the most startling so far. Legere, he said, had accidentally admitted to him that he had taken part in the attack.

Late in 1986 Legere had asked for a meeting with Johnston. They met on January 2, 1987, at Dorchester Penitentiary, near Moncton, just a few days before the trial was set to start. Once his cuffs were removed, Legere checked the room, looking for microphones. He kicked open a drawer and there was a tape recorder in it, much to Johnston's own surprise.

Eventually, Legere satisfied himself that the room was safe. He sat down and started talking. He wanted to make a deal. He hadn't killed anyone, he said. He would tell the truth, testify against Matchett and Curtis, plead guilty, and face a sentence of ten years.

He hadn't even been there that night, Legere told Johnston. It was Matchett, Curtis and a mysterious third guy.

"This third person stayed outside and only came inside after a big fuckup," Legere said. "But this third person only stayed in the background. Scott had problems with the old man. He got away and went outside or stumbled."

That's when Curtis hit John Glendenning with the gun. Talk about a rock was "bull." They had to drag Glendenning back into the house. "He was staggering, and this time Curtis told the old man they would rape his wife if he didn't open the safe." John turned the dial but couldn't get the safe to open. Mary was untied and dragged upstairs. She couldn't open it either.

"Curtis hit the old man and tied him up in the same room as the safe. Curtis told this third person that the old man was not breathing."

Legere's description fit with what the police knew, but he was making a key mistake: in his excitement, he was slipping into the first person. "I parked behind the rec centre," he told Johnston when he described the failed attack on the Wednesday before the murder.

The mistakes grew more frequent as Legere recounted what happened next to John and Mary. "I took a garbage can and I put water on his face," Legere told Johnston. John came to – he wasn't dead. "Curtis and Matchett were so much in a frenzy I had to holler, I had to scream at them twice so they would stop hitting the old woman."

Then Legere regained control and switched back to the third person.

The mysterious third man told them to take the safe.

Curtis screamed at Mary, "You old bag. We're going to burn the house down with you in it." The third guy told him to cool it and went to get the car.

Legere had told Johnston all this to show he really wanted a deal. "Allan said again that if he could get ten years, he'd be out in seven. He would have to serve this time in solitary, as he would testify. He said he would do hard time in the pen and after seven years he would go to Afghanistan to live the rest of his life there."

Johnston's testimony was interrupted by a shouted curse from Legere. Johnston pressed on.

Legere had insisted throughout their meeting that he was innocent. "I didn't kill anybody," he had said, "but I feel partly responsible for the death of the old man. I still feel responsible. I was sick to my stomach after I learned that he was dead. Those fucking idiots, Curtis and Matchett. I'm no killer. It was supposed to be a safe attack."

On January 18, Legere's ex-girl friend Christine Searle took the stand wearing hot-pink pants, white ankle boots, and a white pullover. Her bleached-blonde hair was swept back from her face, and large sunglasses hid her eyes.

Yes, theirs had been a stormy relationship, she acknowledged. They fought most of the time. And though they had talked about getting married, Searle insisted she would never have married Legere.

She had spent much of June 21 – the day of the attack at the Glendenning home – with Legere. He left early in the evening and didn't return to her Chatham apartment until four in the morning.

"I heard my bathroom going. I woke up. He came in my bedroom. He had nothing on and he said something like 'We have it made now' and threw some money on my bed. He told me to count it. I asked him where he got it. He told me to count it again, so I counted it, and it counted $14,000. It was all in $100 Canadian bills and one $1,000 Canadian bill."

Legere took the money, bundled it up with an elastic, and jammed it in the pocket of a pair of jogging pants. "I asked him where he got the money again. Mr. Legere told me that him and some friends had planned a robbery, but that his friends had done it, that he was not there, nor was he near the property when this happened.

"I asked him who his friends were. He told me it was Scott Curtis, Todd Matchett, and another man from Saint John, but he wouldn't tell me who it was. And he told me Curtis and Matchett beat the people very badly, that they were an elderly couple. He said he told them to call an ambulance for them and they refused, and they gave him a share of the money because he knew about the robbery and when it was going to happen. Legere told me that there was $45,000 in the safe and they split it three ways." (Later reports put the figure as high as $100,000. Slightly more than $20,000 was recovered.)

Legere and Searle fell asleep. Sunday morning, Searle asked him if the old woman had been raped. Legere said no, but that Curtis had sexually assaulted her with a weapon. Legere took a dishcloth from the sink in her apartment and began to wipe his black leather jacket, which was draped over a chair. It was a habit of his. He took good care of it, always keeping it in the back seat of his car if he wasn't wearing it. This would be a key point in the trial.

Christine asked a boy from downstairs to come up. She wanted him to run out and buy her a pack of cigarettes. "I asked Allan for a dollar. He gave it to me, then he threw the little boy out of the apartment and grabbed the dollar from me. There were dark red-brown stains on it, and Allan turned on the burner on my stove and burned it. He said it didn't look good."

David Hughes entered a seven-page letter from Searle as evidence in an effort to discredit her. "I want you back in my arms, in my bed, in my life," it read in part. "God I really do miss you. I feel empty inside. I know I'll never find anyone in my lifetime to take the place of Big Al. No one could or would ever get that close to me. You're the only one to break my barriers. You are the only one. You are the only man I wanted to stay with.

"No one talks to me now, not a God damn soul, unless it's getting information about you. By the way, the hitchhiker you picked up has been interested in your well being. She isn't the only one, but I won't go on about that slut you have been . . . behind my back. Whatever you were getting, I was probably getting more than you."

Legere burst out laughing at that. Judge Paul Godin, however, was not amused. "This is not being done for entertainment," he warned.

Searle defended her actions by saying that she wrote the letter while on nerve pills.

There was still nearly a week to go in the trial, but already three witnesses had placed Legere at the scene of the murder. The next morning, an expert witness added physical evidence to the mounting case against Legere.

Duff Evers of the RCMP laboratory in Sackville, New Brunswick, told the court that a hair found on the face of John Glendenning matched Legere's. As well, hair from Mary Glendenning was found in the zipper of Legere's leather jacket. (Legere later argued that he had loaned the jacket to Matchett and Curtis and that it was returned to him after the Glendenning episode.)

Evers's testimony that Tuesday morning marked the end of the Crown's case. It was now Legere's turn.

Legere had a reputation among lawyers for being a difficult client to control. He often refused to take their advice and had sued at least one whom he felt had not done his job properly. He lived up to that reputation on January 19, when he took the stand. He insisted on testifying – a position his lawyer had counselled against. However, Legere was betting on his ability to convince people to believe him. He was hoping he could sway a jury of Miramichiers untrained in the law that he was not guilty.

Crown prosecutor Fred Ferguson remembered one incident that afternoon which, for him, set the tone for everything that followed.

The witness box is in front of the jury and to the immediate left of the judge. If the judge and witness stretch out their arms, they could touch fingertips. "The judge had his water glass positioned on the left side of his desk, in front of him," Ferguson recalled. "He'd been sitting there with his water glass for two and a half weeks, drinking away. When Legere went into the box, he kind of looked around the courtroom, reached over and took the judge's water glass, and drank it. He completely upended the courtroom with one small, incidental act. It was audacious. Audacity is Mr. Legere's byline."

Legere's decision to testify was not a great surprise to Ferguson. He had prosecuted Legere often through the years and knew how he worked. "He had quite an aura about him in court. He was very much part of his own defence. He made, I think, input into a number of the large decisions that were made by Mr. Hughes – who worked alone on this trial."

Legere's defence was simple: everyone who testified against him was lying. He had nothing to do with planning the Glendenning attack. He first heard about the safe from a local businessman who asked him if he was interested in a quick fifteen or twenty thousand dollars. He thought little more of it, although he did mention it to Todd's father, Billy, a short time later, near the end of May.

There had been *two* failed attempts to steal from the safe before the June 21 killing, according to Legere. He drove Langan, Matchett, and Curtis to Black River Bridge on June 11 and dropped them off. When he went back for them a short time later, he found them on the side of the road hitchhiking.

They tried again two days later, he said. This time he parked behind the nearby community centre. When he had grown tired of waiting, he drove by the house, blew his horn when he could see no sign of them, then drove back to his hiding place. Finally, he gave up and took off back to Chatham. He met Langan the next day. "I told him, 'I just got out of prison and I'm not going back for any money.'" That was the last he had to do with the store or the three men, Legere told the court.

The next time he had anything to do with the case was around two-thirty in the morning of June 22, several hours after the Glendenning attack. He was staying at Christine Searle's apartment and heard a car pull up beside the building. Looking out the window, he recognized the car, so he went down to talk to the occupants.

He recognized two of the men, but didn't know the third man, who was supposedly from Saint John.

There were plastic bags full of money on the floor of the car and a pair of coveralls and sneakers, both covered in blood, in the back seat. They handed Legere a bundle of money and described what had happened.

John Glendenning had been impossible to handle. He had run out the door and hit his head on the ground. They had to drag him back inside. "They told me they tied them up and untied them," Legere confessed. "Neither one would open the safe. They slapped them a bit. After it was over, they rolled the safe downstairs and away they went. They said they were not dead or anything. They said the old guy was knocked out and they said, 'I poured water over him.'"

He had offered to call an ambulance in case the old man had suffered a heart attack, Legere told the court, but the three men told him no because they might get caught in a roadblock.

It was true that he showed the money to Christine, but she counted it on her own – he didn't have to ask. He couldn't even remember touching it. He did burn a stained bill because he was worried about what people seeing it might say, but the stain was rust, not blood. And it was Christine who hid the money, not him.

And as for Mason Johnston, well, he had lied on the stand to help put him away, Legere suggested. In fact, it was Johnston who had suggested the deal, not him. "I told him I would plead guilty to a ten-year term, that I would probably get ten years just for knowing about it. I said I'd probably be out in seven years and go to live in Ontario. Mason told me he talked to Fred Ferguson, but because the public was watching, they couldn't be too lenient. He said they talked to Mrs. Glendenning and they knew that it was the young guys who beat them and that the third guy stayed in the background. Johnston said he'd tell the judge the third guy didn't do nothing."

"Were you in Black River Bridge on June 21 or June 22?" Hughes asked his client as he wrapped up his questioning.

"Nowhere near it," Legere responded.

"Did you kill John Glendenning?"

"No, sir, I didn't."

It had been a remarkable performance. Remarkable, but unconvincing.

It's difficult to say what might have happened if Legere had admitted to being present, but not involved in the beatings. The jury might have believed him. But his decision to deny any involvement probably hampered his defence.

"In the end, he didn't help his case," Ferguson later argued. "His explanation was fairly weak. He was asking the jurors to buy the story that he'd gotten $15,000 from the robbery and murder of John Glendenning because he knew about it, because he'd participated in the planning of a routine break and enter, as he called it. That the people who'd perpetrated the crime all of a sudden had come to his door and given him one-third of the money that was allegedly taken in the robbery-murder. It made no sense."

The facts were clear as far as Ferguson was concerned. Legere was guilty. "Our position right through this was there was absolutely no question what the intention was once they got inside the house and started beating the Glendennings. All you had to do was go back and look at the photographs, the brutality, listen to the medical evidence from the doctors, the pathologists, and the way they beat these people.

"No one in their right mind can imagine that there was anything less than the intention to kill here. The brutality was that monstrous."

The jury's decision came quickly. They began considering the case Thursday evening at 6:20. After breaking to sleep, they announced the next morning that they had decided. Just before 10:30, the jury filed into the courtroom. Juror Gary Williston was carrying in his left hand the sheet of paper with the decision on it.

Mr. Justice Godin asked him if the jury had reached a verdict. Yes, came the reply.

What is it? Godin asked.

"Guilty."

Hughes requested that each juror be asked individually for his or her verdict. Each answered loudly and clearly. Only Wally Jimmo had trouble. When his turn came, his voice failed him. "Guilty," he said, his voice barely a squeak.

Legere was sentenced to life in prison for committing second-degree murder. He would have no chance of parole for eighteen years.

He would appeal, he vowed to reporters as he was taken down the courthouse steps at noon and put into a waiting car. Well over a hundred people were there to watch him leave. Among them were about a dozen schoolchildren, mostly girls, shouting at Legere from across the car to which he was being led. He ignored them as he got in, but suddenly turned and through the window stared in their direction before turning again and looking straight ahead. The car pulled away.

SIX

"The Devil in his Eyes"

THOSE WHO know Allan Legere always mention one thing about him: he loves being in the spotlight.

Whatever he does, he must be the focus of attention. Fate seemed to understand that need right from the beginning. Legere was born on February 13, 1948 – Friday the thirteenth. Years later, fascinated by numbers and their significance, Legere would tell people he weighed thirteen pounds at birth.

A photograph of Legere from September 1955 shows him posed with his classmates. Two things stand out. First, the seven-year-old Legere was a cute boy with a pixie-like face. Second, it's impossible to miss him. The other children stand prim and erect, looking straight ahead, trying to smile for the camera while dutifully waiting to be told when they can move. Legere's head is turned slightly to the right and down, his distinctive pale blue eyes peeking at the camera from beneath a shock of dark hair falling over his face. Instead of a smile, there is an engaging smirk.

Later in life, Legere recognized this need to be seen and remembered. In the 1970s he wrote a letter to a

Chatham newspaper in which he described the world as he saw it. It is composed of two kinds of people, he said, the pirates and the sheep. The sheep live inside the law and do what they're told, enjoying the safety they think that brings. The pirates, however, understand what's really happening and refuse to go along. They live outside the law, or on the risky edges of society. Most people are sheep. Few are destined to be pirates. Allan Legere said he preferred piracy to dutiful obedience.

Legere's birthdate may have set him apart from the crowd, but his early life offered little hope for a bright future. He was born illegitimate in Chatham Head, the last in a poor family of four children. In the 1950s, Chatham Head was a tough place in which to grow up. Some homes were mere shacks. The community was huddled in what was essentially a white ghetto on low-lying land across the Miramichi River from Newcastle.

There was a stigma attached to being from Chatham Head then. You were made fun of by the other kids at school, teased about the second-hand clothes with the obvious patches. People said "Chatham Head" as if the words themselves were unclean. The tight-knit community had a reputation for being dangerous after dark. Back then, Chatham Head was a place to get out of as quickly as possible.

Even the teachers at the Chatham Head School knew the score, recalled a woman who went to school with Legere. "We were at the bottom and yet there were places poorer than us. We knew some of the teachers wanted to leave as fast as they could. The kids from Chatham Head were looked down upon, and I always thought it was discrimination."

It was doubly difficult for the young Legere. Like

many others, his family struggled to make do on the $88 a month Vince Legere made after he went to war with thousands of others in the 1940s. But unlike many, Vince chose not to return after the war to pick up the strands of his life. He moved to Halifax instead, abandoning his family.

Allan Legere, in fact, wasn't really a Legere at all. He was the offspring of Lionel Comeau, whom Louise Legere had taken up with after her husband's desertion. Little is known about Comeau, whose identity Legere was to learn of only years later. He was known as a vicious drunk. One story has him hacking his way through Louise's front door with an axe after she had locked him out. Whatever his character, Comeau didn't stay with Louise long. She raised her children herself.

Louise was well known for speaking her mind and living her life as she saw fit, whatever the neighbours might say. Living common law with a man was not done in that day, but she did it.

Allan Legere is remembered as a bright student with plenty of potential. "Allan should have been sitting in Parliament today, not running away," a childhood acquaintance said years later.

Descriptions of him as a child vary. A former teacher and school principal said, "He was never a bad boy, never a saucy boy." She once gave him two dollars so he could take the high school entrance exam in nearby Newcastle. He ran all the way to Newcastle, more than half a mile away, and scored 75 percent. A friend remembered him as an unfailingly polite boy. "He had the cutest fleck of black hair and he was so shy and polite, always yes ma'am, yes sir. Oh, sometimes he could be a bully, pulling girls' hats off and throwing them and stuff. But all the little boys were like that."

Not everyone has such fond memories of the young Legere. "He was a bad little bastard," said one woman who grew up with him. "He was always throwing stones. You'd be out on the street, he'd wave and smile at you, and as soon as your back was turned, he'd throw stones at you."

Tragedy struck the Legeres in 1956, when Allan was just eight. His older brother Freddy, a soldier, was struck by a car while he and two friends were walking three abreast one night. They had just crossed the Morrissy Bridge, which connects Newcastle with Chatham Head, when the car came from behind and ran over them, killing Freddy and one of the others. The family would maintain that the case was covered up because they didn't have the money to push for justice. Years later Louise Legere would tell Allan: "I wished you'da died instead of Freddy."

Legere developed what would become a lifelong passion for weightlifting when he hit junior high school. By then he was at Harkins Junior and Senior High School in Newcastle. It was a better-equipped facility than those in Chatham Head, with the region's first and only set of weights in its gym. Legere was conscientious about his workouts, pumping iron at least three mornings a week, rising early to get to school by 7:45. There was no one to show him what to do, so he devised his own training system, using whatever books he could find as guidance. "He was always alone, but he didn't mind asking for help," a teacher recalled.

Still, Legere had a tough time at school. He failed Grade 9 twice, dropping out partway through his second attempt. The curious walk he was known for – erect, chest puffed out – began to take on a definite swagger. By age sixteen, he had developed a love for breaking into homes, not so much to steal – although he certainly did that – as to demonstrate his ability to move through a home undetected by its occupants. It was something to do, he shrugged.

In 1964, he was fined $15 and spent fifteen days in jail for theft. Two years later it was theft over $50 and an eighteen-month sentence.

There also was an element of the Peeping Tom to Legere's escapades. He would brag about slipping into motel rooms to caress women as they slept unawares. "That's how slick I am," he chuckled.

In his book *The Encyclopedia of Human Behavior*, psychologist Robert Goldenson speaks of the voyeur as being "typically an isolated, shy individual who fears women and doubts his sexual adequacy. Peeping gives him satisfaction without risk of rejection or failure. It also reassures his potency. In addition, it probably serves as an outlet for aggressive, hostile drives, since peeping is a stealthy act and probably makes the voyeur feel superior to those he is watching." Goldenson adds that the typical peeper "is not criminally inclined and seldom attacks women." However, "in rare instances, voyeurs have been known to develop into rapists and arsonists."

By the late 1960s, Legere had married a woman named Marilyn and moved to North Bay, Ontario, where he worked as a machinist. He had a gift for it, particularly when it came to cars. He returned to the Miramichi in 1972 and was employed as a machinist at a pulp mill, but it didn't work out. Arrested for possession of stolen goods, he was sentenced to five months in prison. When he went back to the mill, he said, "the dogs gave me labor work and a greenhorn took my machinist position."

Legere returned to a life of crime. Said a friend: "He figured that was the only way he could survive." Legere also began to experiment with drugs and to cultivate an interest in Satanism and demonology. His behaviour became increasingly erratic and reckless.

When the RCMP managed to stop him following a car chase in 1972, he yelled at them, "Don't touch my body! Don't touch my body!" Once police had him in handcuffs, he calmly asked, "Don't you think my body is beautiful?"

Sculpted by almost ten years of weight-training, his physique had become an obsession. He showered several times a day, maintaining a regime of cleanliness that could only be deemed fanatical.

Paroled in 1973, Legere dwelled on slights, real and imagined, he had endured. "Me pay for anything?" he snorted. "I've been paying all my life."

Once, he walked into a Baptist church during Sunday service wearing nothing but cutoff jeans. He told stunned worshippers that they were all going to hell because he was Jesus Christ and they could not get to heaven but through him. (Years later he railed against the hypocrisy of organized religion. "Samson killed 100s of bastards of Romans . . . and is a biblical hero. St. Pat persecuted Christians and looted churches . . . Now people pray to his little statues." Lucifer, he wrote, was "God's chief angel before the fall. Lucifer is very powerful since nobody believes in him anymore. Only when they are scared do they pray.")

Despite these actions, some continued to believe that Legere was fundamentally a decent person. By most accounts, he was a good husband to Marilyn and a doting father to their two children. At least in the beginning. A friend blamed drugs for Legere's fall. "You know, he had a good heart. If you were stuck on the side of the road and your car was broke down and it was raining, he'd stop and help you out, even if he didn't know you. He wouldn't leave anybody stuck."

Give him drugs, however, and "he'd dream he was a superpower with the attitude that 'I can do what I want to do.' Once he got into the drugs he didn't care what he done. He'd break and enter more, just go crazy."

Few marriages can withstand such a lifestyle, and Legere's was no exception. As his relationship with Marilyn soured, he started to see other women. Eventually, his wife left him, taking their son and daughter with her to Ottawa.

A former friend said that Legere "liked dating girls, liked hanging around girls." But for all his self-proclaimed stature as a ladies' man, Legere also viewed women as objects of abuse and scorn.

In 1974 he was brought in for questioning about the murder of Chatham Head resident Beatrice Mary Redmond, who had been stabbed nearly eighty times and left at her doorstep after coming home from church. Police interrogated Legere for eighteen hours, but had to let him go. There was nothing to hold him on. The questioning had been so long and detailed that police looking through a one-way window into the interrogation room said *they* were ready to confess to the murder just to get it over with.

Legere was also named as a suspect in a case where the head of a corpse buried in a crypt had been hacked off and dropped on a man's doorstep. No charges were laid, however.

During this time Legere developed a reputation as a fighter. "When he fights, he fights seriously," a friend recalled. "He'd tear a guy's eye out if he had to. He doesn't care. He believes in surviving. When it comes to fighting, he's a vicious fighter. He doesn't like to lose. He fought with a lot of people and he could fight, but he was dirty. He'd hit you from behind, hit you whichever way he could. He believed in winning."

While working as a longshoreman on the Newcastle docks, Legere got into a fight with a coworker. After knocking his opponent down, Legere grabbed a peavey, a long wooden pole with a metal hook at the end used by loggers. "Allan was going to drive that peavey into him when three of us jumped him," a friend recounted. "He woulda killed the fellow for sure."

"If there's such a thing as being born bad, he was born bad."

By the late 1970s, Legere was working as the manager of Chatham's Zodiac Club, a place notorious for fights, even shootings, in its parking lot. A 1978 letter to the Chatham newspaper described the atmosphere of the club: "Last week," it read, "a friend of ours went to the Zodiac alone and got a bit drunk and was ready to pass out. He was promptly picked up, thrown downstairs, dragged outside and beaten. This lad was not even causing any trouble. A few people went down to see why they did it and they were jumped by people with bats, tire wrenches and guns. One lad has some 20 stitches on the top of his head to prove it."

"Remember our slogan," the letter concluded, "tit for tat, shoot my dog, I'll kill your cat."

Booze and drugs ended Legere's career at the Zodiac. Late one April night he shoved his way into the sound booth of the disco and forcibly kissed the young female disc jockey. When she resisted, he grabbed her between the legs with one hand and ripped her sweater and tore at her bra with the other. Legere was sentenced to thirty days in jail. He subsequently wrote the woman a letter of apology, saying he had been taking drugs at the time of the assault.

On another occasion, when a woman refused to dance with him, Legere spit in her face. In a third incident, he ordered a woman to dance with him. When she declined, he pulled her onto the dance floor, grabbed her by the crotch, twirled her around, and said, "Dance when I say dance!"

In 1979 Legere had yet another run-in with police. He was drinking heavily that year. One night during a fight, he drove a broken beer bottle into the man's face and twisted it. Several weeks later he was drinking in a Chatham club, known locally as the Wing. When he grabbed a beer belonging to another man, the man snatched it back. Legere responded by breaking a glass and charging. An off-duty policeman working as a bouncer grabbed a pool cue and smashed it across Legere's face, breaking his jaw.

Chatham police chief Dan Allen rode with Legere in the ambulance to Moncton. "We talked all the way down, just general conversation. He asked me why I was coming. 'To look after you,' I told him."

The two men had an understanding, said Allen, now retired because of back problems, but known in his day as a tough cop who brooked no nonsense. "He knew what I would do if I had to do it. Somehow he respected me for that. He would never have talked to me at length if he hadn't."

Legere, he said, was a loner in his crimes. "A lone man is hard to get. Nobody to talk on him. Nobody to tell stories, and only himself knows what he's achieved and what he hasn't."

"He was good. I hate to give him credit for anything.

But to give the devil his due, he was the best I ever run up against, and I've run up against a lot of criminals," Allen said.

"His personality could change from one extreme to the other. He can turn himself on, turn himself off. Never sit still for five minutes, gone here, gone there. A wheeler and a dealer."

Before Legere was transferred to Moncton that night, he was taken to Chatham police headquarters for booking. While there he pulled a knife on an officer. He was subsequently charged with possession of a weapon dangerous to the public peace. Acquittal followed, but the Crown later appealed and won.

It was during that appeal hearing that Legere had the opportunity to show another side of his personality, namely that of the persuasive talker. Before his sentencing, Legere, not his lawyer, addressed the three Court of Appeal judges. He was after a lighter sentence. By all accounts it was a brilliant forty-five-minute discourse on how the system had abused him, how the community blamed him for all the crimes on the Miramichi, how it hated him and was out to get him.

It seemed to work. Legere was sentenced to a twenty-four-month term, far less than what the Crown wanted.

Fred Ferguson was the Crown prosecutor handling the case. When the court recessed that day, the clerk of the court – who had the ear of the judges – came up to him. "You know, that guy gave some kind of speech. It was very effective, because I understand the sentence the court handed out was not the one they had in mind when they came in here this morning."

Legere didn't return to the Miramichi when he was released from jail. He moved to Moncton. Sporting a ponytail, he would go to auctions in the city's East End to get furniture for the apartment he shared with his new wife, the former Donna O'Toole.

Trouble seemed to dog him even when he wasn't looking for it. One Tuesday night, he was standing by the canteen at the back of an auction hall trying to see what was going on. When some local toughs stood in front of him, blocking his view, he politely asked them to move.

"They thought he was an easy punching bag," recalled an observer. "One of the thugs gave Allan a sucker punch in the nose. Worst mistake he made. Next thing you know, Allan knocked him out cold." The toughs took off.

Eventually, Allan and Donna Legere moved out of their apartment to a mobile home in the city's West End. Things were a little rough between them: he would beat her occasionally; neighbours would see her with a black eye.

In the summer of 1982, Moncton was plagued by a series of burglaries. Someone very skilful was entering homes, stealing valuables, cutting underwear off women while they slept. The break-ins continued through the summer, with the police trying to track their elusive prey with dogs.

Finally, the police found their thief in late August. Cornered in his trailer, Allan Legere wriggled through a small window and started to run. A police bullet to his lower back prevented the escape. Later he sued the police department over this episode. The case is still before the courts.

During the subsequent jury trial, two witnesses – a husband and wife – couldn't be present to testify as to who had broken into their home. The Crown wished to read into the court record the couple's evidence from the preliminary hearing. Legere did not. He also opposed any adjournment that would allow the witnesses time to show up.

The judge allowed the adjournment anyway. At that point, Legére stood in the prisoner's dock, pulled out a hidden razor and slashed both wrists. "That's what I think of this!" he shouted.

Blood poured down Legere's arms. The judge pounded on his desk with his gavel. Jurors screamed. And a distraught court stenographer bolted from the room.

Two days later, Legere was back, his wrists bandaged. He soon realized he'd made a mistake in blocking use of evidence from the preliminary hearing. Had he allowed that testimony, the court would have heard from only the wife. The delay had allowed the husband to take the stand as well.

Yes, the husband said, he remembered seeing Legere in his house.

How could he be so sure?

"I'll never forget those eyes."

They are pale blue. A person who once babysat his children recalled, "There was just something about the eyes that made you feel uneasy, not unfriendly, just different."

"I figgered the devil is right in his eyes," asserted Billy Matchett, father of Todd Matchett. According to his own reckoning, he has known Legere for about twenty-five years, and it's the eyes that stick in his memory. "He's got the most dangerous eyes I've ever seen on a human being. He can look right through a box, right through you. He has that stare."

Legere got three years for the break into the couple's home. It meant he would have to go to federal prison for the first time.

Dorchester is a maximum-security institution, more than a century old, and it sits like a fortress on a hill in southeastern New Brunswick. Legere played the system there well enough to secure a transfer to Springhill medium-security prison in Nova Scotia. But he muscled other inmates there, pushed drugs, fought, and spent time in solitary confinement. After just two months, he was sent back to Dorchester.

Released on parole, mandatory supervision, in 1985, Legere returned to Moncton to discover that his wife, fed up with his behaviour and scared, had left after selling both the mobile home and his car. Legere was furious: to lose a woman was one thing; to lose a beloved car was an insult of a different order.

Understandably, Moncton police didn't want to see Legere back in town. Police in Chatham and Newcastle told the parole board that he was dangerous and violent, that people in the area were afraid.

The day of his release, Legere went to visit police chief Dan Allen at his home, vowing that things would be different this time. Allen remembered, "He said, 'I want to go straight and I'll never bother your town again.' I told him, 'No matter where you do something, I'll let police know.' You knew it was just con talk. I knew he wouldn't outfox me."

Legere's version of the conversation was quite different. "I assured him to keep his men off my back and I'll stay clean. Chief Allen said, 'You'll never make it on the Miramichi, since your name is notorious.'"

And Legere didn't make it. He wanted the big score too much. That's always been his dream, to make the big score and leave, move to someplace exotic. That's why he, along with Matchett and Curtis, robbed and killed John Glendenning and left his wife for dead.

Legere maintains his innocence in that murder. At his "kangaroo trial," as he called it, he denied being at the Glendenning residence the night of the attack. However, in a letter written in December 1989, he admitted that he had taken part in the robbery but denied any participation in the beatings. That "fact," he insisted, should absolve him from any blame for the murder he was convicted of committing.

The New Brunswick Court of Appeal didn't see it his way. It said Legere ran the show. "The evidence indicates that the third man, who may not have actually inflicted any blows, aided Curtis and Matchett by directing them and actually took Mrs. Glendenning upstairs to try to open the safe. The third man instructed Matchett and Curtis to take the safe away to be opened later and generally supervised the activities." That third man, the court said, was one Allan Legere. It threw out his appeal.

Back in prison at the start of his life term for the Glendenning murder, Legere spent months in solitary confinement, refusing to come out even for the one hour of exercise permitted daily. He stopped lifting weights; his body turned flabby.

Perhaps he was on edge from the knifing episode that had occurred the previous November when he was awaiting trial in the Glendenning case. At that time he had spread the word through the prison community that he hadn't beaten the Glendennings; Todd Matchett and Scott Curtis had.

Longtime inmates of Dorchester told Curtis and Matchett that Legere was setting them up, shafting them. A guard recalled the situation this way: "When Matchett and Curtis came in, these guys were all a piece of shit. They were nothing, just punks. They'd never been in prison before. The other guys they see these new guys come in, well, that's their meat for a while."

One day Legere went to the Dorchester gym. Curtis was there. "They waited for a shiv, it was there," the guard said, "and Legere was stabbed. Legere wanted to prove he was a strong man. He was. When he came out of the gym, he walked to the hospital. Superman."

The blade punctured Legere's lung. In the process all three inmates had proved a point in the fiercely hierarchical world of prison. "Matchett and Curtis had proved they weren't rats and hadn't raped anybody," said the guard. Legere, by walking out under his own power, had created a myth of invincibility. Curtis was charged with the stabbing, but Legere wouldn't testify against his former accomplice and the charge was dropped.

Following the Glendenning trial, Legere fed off his hatred for those whom he felt had unjustly put him away. In 1989 he said of Crown prosecutor Fred Ferguson: "I despise [him] for what he did . . . Everybody who has wronged me in any way always pays the price, for that is the law of the universe . . . I swear, all who have judged me will be judged by their own measures."

Although Ferguson prosecuted Legere time and again for more than a decade, he says he's still not sure what makes his long-time adversary tick.

There's Allan Legere the religious fanatic who can talk about Jesus and the devil for hours. There's the smooth, articulate, convincing con man. There's the petty criminal with a talent for cat burglary. And then there's the hard-nosed, brutal man, "a man with a very violent streak in him who can bring terror to people's eyes just by the mention of his name. What sets him apart from the rest is that he plays a brilliant game of cat and mouse in the way he commits his crimes, when he escapes, when police try to catch him. He's had a lot of experience at it. There's a side to him that's a little bit bizarre. Add a dash of that to any criminal, you have the makings of a fellow who stands a cut above the rest."

To this day, Legere dreams of other places, other lands, the Arctic, Iran and Afghanistan. He identifies himself with the oppressed; he sees himself as a Don Quixote tilting at society's windmills. A talented artist who developed a knack for illustrating in junior high school, he cites Picasso's famous sketch of Don Quixote and Sancho Panza as one of his favourite works of art. He even painted his own version of the Quixote character once and gave it to his parole officer.

While he was in prison in Dorchester, he sent a lawyer a hand-drawn Christmas card. In one panel Santa Claus was shown with an empty bag going down a chimney. In the next there was Santa coming up the chimney, his bag full. The caption read, "Ho! Ho! Ho!"

Legere has a "fondness" for conspiracies. In his life they have stretched from the steps of the courthouse in Newcastle to the gates of the Supreme Court in Ottawa. Everyone except Allan Legere is to blame for Allan Legere's troubles. Police plant his hair at crime scenes. They lie under oath to put him behind bars. His family is harassed. The community hates and misunderstands him, imprisons him for crimes he could not possibly have committed. Appeal courts don't "do dick for me, so if you take my life, I'll fight."

It's always been that way for Allan Legere. Them against him, a daredevil who, for all his smarts and love of the limelight, always seems to end up the loser, always seems to be denied the place in society that he believes is his by right.

SEVEN

Escape

ITS OFFICIAL name is the Atlantic Institution. But most people – except the bureaucrats in the Correctional Service of Canada – call it Renous, after the village where it's located, twenty miles southeast of Newcastle on the road to Fredericton.

It's a maximum-security prison. Opened early in 1987, it cost more than $60 million to build. It has the most modern security facilities, two sets of wire fences topped with razor-ribbon wire, which could cut a man to bits if he ever tried to climb over. And even if he succeeded, the sensing monitors between the fences would detect him. So would the cameras that constantly sweep the area.

Still, in its short life, there have been strikes by inmates, protests by employees who said the institution was so badly run it was a dangerous place to work, several wardens – and one escape.

But Inmate 112120A didn't escape over the fences. He used the human defects in the security system to make his getaway.

Allan Legere is a cunning con artist. He had, a report

on his escape said in its officialese, "the verbal communication skills necessary to 'play the system' and has been quite adept at doing so." During his stay at Renous, to which he had been transferred from Dorchester in 1987, Legere was "always very cooperative . . . quite polite and staff [did] not mind talking with Legere on a regular basis due to these factors."

It also became apparent, much too late of course, that the prison staff didn't consider him "very dangerous," unlike the police and the community, who knew him all too well.

Faced with a man adept at manipulating people, and guards lax in following procedure, the prison was ready for a fall.

Legere often complained of an ear infection and on several occasions was taken to Moncton to be treated by a specialist. On the morning of Wednesday, May 3, 1989, he was taken yet again. Within hours he was a man on the run. Within seven months, he was a prime suspect in four brutal murders and one of the most infamous criminals in Canada.

Shortly before seven that Wednesday morning, guards Robert Winters and Robert Hazlett were told that they were taking Legere to the Dr. Georges Dumont Hospital in Moncton.

Minutes later, Winters went to Unit 3, Range C, Cell 3 to inform Legere. Then Winters left, returning about fifty minutes later with Hazlett. Legere was on the toilet. He told them he wanted more time. They agreed and left, returning ten minutes later.

They handcuffed Legere and started towards the steel exit door. Legere announced that he'd forgotten his watch. He needed it, he said, and insisted on returning for it. They did. It took three or four minutes to find it. It was behind Legere's television.

The trio left again, this time going through the barrier. Then Legere had another demand: he wanted to exchange his cell slippers for his sneakers. Winters and Hazlett again acquiesced and returned Legere to his cell. Legere also wanted a newspaper to do the crossword puzzle and two Old Port cigars, even though he didn't smoke.

In the admission and discharge area, Legere was taken to a strip-search cell. His handcuffs were removed. Legere stripped. The A&D officer came into the room. The bearded inmate looked at him and asked sarcastically: "Do you want to see my prick too?"

The officer left and the strip search began. The guards looked in Legere's "mouth, ears, nose, under his armpits, the soles of his feet, the hair on his head, [and we made] him spread the cheeks of his behind."

The guards, though, did not use a hand scanner similar to those used at airports. If they had, the scanner would have sounded for Legere, it was later discovered, had hidden a collapsed TV antenna in his rectum.

Once Legere was dressed, the guards put a body chain with handcuffs on him, strapped leg irons around his ankles, draped his parka over his shoulders, then buttoned it at the neck and bottom. His hands were out of sight.

They left for Moncton, a two-hour drive. No one called the Moncton city police, as they were required to, to tell them that they were bringing in a dangerous criminal. It would prove a costly oversight.

When the prison van entered Moncton, it headed away from the specialist's office. An upset Legere told the guards that they had missed the turn. The guards explained that he would see the specialist at the Dumont Hospital, not at his office as had happened on other occasions. Clearly, Legere had planned to escape from the doctor's office, a locale he knew well. Now he would be forced to improvise.

At the hospital, Legere said he needed to go to the washroom. Winters went with him and opened the men's bathroom door to see if there was any other way out. There wasn't. Legere went in, then peeked out the door to ask for toilet paper. Seconds later he burst from the room. His body chain was gone. So were the handcuffs and leg irons. (Guards later found one of the cigars broken in two in prison van. It's believed Legere had hidden a makeshift key in it.)

Winters was stunned. Legere ran down the corridor and through the hospital doors, Winters chasing him. A nurse ran up to Hazlett, standing near another washroom, and said in French, "Your prisoner's escaped!" Hazlett ran.

Outside, the prison van driver saw Legere running and started after him. Legere jumped over a railing and turned to slash at the driver with the TV antenna. "Stay the fuck away," he yelled.

Winters arrived with a can of Mace in his hand. But the disabling spray only caught Legere on his shoulder.

In the meantime, the van driver called Renous to report the escape. Moncton police still hadn't been notified. It was 10:40.

In a nearby parking lot, Peggy Olive, who worked for the local SPCA, was waiting to pay her ticket. Suddenly her car door flew open. "He told me to move over. I just did not move. He had what looked like a screwdriver in his hand. He pushed me and half sat on me."

With Legere at the wheel, they rammed through the exit barrier. Olive was terrified. "He told me he was doing eighteen years for murder. He had nothing to lose." Legere told her to contact a CBC reporter he knew so he could say he hadn't killed anyone.

An empty cat cage separated Olive and Legere. It bothered him, and he kept trying to throw it in the back seat. Olive moved it.

Legere's personality kept changing in the car. "He was very aggressive. Then he wanted to be a good guy. He kept changing from the good guy to the bad guy."

Legere soon dropped Olive off, but kept her car. Olive ran into an optical store to call police.

Legere left Olive's car in the parking lot of AM radio station CKCW, in the city's upper-middle-class West End. He grabbed her blue ultrasuede coat and disappeared.

City police were by now on the case. Roadblocks were set up and patrols began. Traffic backed up. The news travelled quickly. In Newcastle, the husband of one of the *Miramichi Leader's* reporters picked up the news on a police scanner and called the paper, where the scanner's reports were played over a loudspeaker. Everything stopped in the office. People stood motionless, unbelieving.

Moncton's West End is part residential, part industrial. First there are houses, then an industrial park surrounded by woods, and, beyond that, at its extreme western edge, is the Gordon Yard, CN's rail-traffic control centre. Close to two thousand railcars pass through there daily. It was an area very familiar to Legere. In the summer of 1982, he had eluded police and their dogs while on a burglary rampage. Police soon concentrated their search in the district.

One night they came close to snaring the escapee. A

police dog had caught his scent as he was running through the woods. A police helicopter was called in, and it's searchlight penetrated the darkness. But then a thick fog rolled in, a light rain started to fall, and the dog lost the scent.

Scenes like this were repeated on several occasions. Every time there was a sighting or possible sighting, each time food was reported stolen, police were there with dogs and a helicopter. But Legere proved an elusive quarry.

On Sunday, May 7, Max Ramsay was shoeing his horses in a barn at the Truro Raceway in Nova Scotia. An attacker jumped the sixty-two-year-old as he concentrated on his work. He was kicked, beaten, and tied up. Sixteen hours later, someone walking along the banks of the Miramichi River near the Morrissy Bridge found Ramsay's wallet floating in the water. Searchers later dragged Ramsay's 1986 Chrysler New Yorker out of the river. It was empty. Ramsay told police that his attacker matched Legere's description. They were doubtful.

On Monday, May 22, a fearful Miramichi resident called police with a sighting. "I know it was Legere. He was cleanshaven, wore a heavy brown winter jacket, and had white highcut sneakers on." Officers from three police forces went after him in the woods off the Kelly and Gordon roads. Again, no luck. This was the area where the Glendennings' safe had been found. Perhaps, some suggested, Legere was back, searching for his money.

Police couldn't be certain just *what* Legere was planning. And strangely, they failed to check for clues in the one place easily available to them – his cell at Renous.

Police, didn't search the cell until months later, shortly before Legere was captured.

It's unclear why. Perhaps, given what they knew about the man, investigators didn't expect to find much. Legere was unlikely to leave behind anything incriminating. At the same time, he had been in segregation for months. That kind of isolation can change a man, change the way he thinks. And Legere was well known for his love of writing letters to newspapers, lawyers, and politicians. There could have been some clue there as to his frame of mind.

With that opportunity ignored, investigators trying to figure out his next move were left to guess just like everyone else. But then, for most people, it didn't matter *why* he was around. Allan Legere had come home. He was out there. Somewhere. And they were scared.

EIGHT

Everyone Knew Annie

FLAM'S GROCERY store was the heart of the Water Street neighbourhood of Chatham. It had been that way since the store opened in the two-storey, century-old house in 1939. It was all because of the tiny woman who sat in the corner on the chair behind the counter.

The store was Annie Flam's life. She would open it at eight each morning and close at eleven each night. The only times she wasn't in the store was when she was out back hanging clothes on the line or upstairs taking care of her ailing mother. When her mother died, Annie kept the room spotless, rather like a shrine. Years ago, Annie would golf with her friends on Wednesday afternoons. But now she was seventy-five and many of her peers were long dead.

With a new decade looming, Flam had been talking of cashing everything in, who she'd give the bedroom set to, who would get the silver. But it was just talk, people said. Annie couldn't, wouldn't give up the store.

When the Flams came to the Miramichi from Montreal in the 1920s, there was a vibrant Jewish community in the region, the largest in New Brunswick. They had their own synagogue. Gradually the families drifted away until, in 1989, fewer than a dozen Jews lived in town. (Annie's cousin Sam Rubenstein remembers in the 1960s, when they couldn't get the 10 men, or *minyan*, required for the evening prayer. They'd bring in a few gentiles in off the street, put yarmulkas on them and say: "Pray with us, and we'll have a poker game after.")

Annie kept a kosher house. She'd bring in special food from Moncton and Montreal and would observe all the Jewish holy days.

She'd get help from sister-in-law Nina, who, while a great cook, had to learn to prepare Jewish dishes. Nina was a Christian. The Jewish community was upset when she married Bernie, Annie's brother, who was as big as Annie was small. But the anger over the mixed marriage gave way with time, especially when the couple had four girls and adopted another.

Bernie owned a furniture store adjacent to the Flam store. He or Nina would often fill in for Annie, especially on golf Wednesdays.

Nina was a hairdresser until she met Bernie, then she stopped working. But she never lost her touch. A neighbour later said, "For forty years I did her sewing, and she did my hair. The first time anyone else ever touched my hair, it was after all *that*."

Bernie and Annie were so close that he built a connecting door between their two homes.

The Flams were popular in Chatham. Bernie, in fact, became mayor of the town, the first Jewish mayor of any municipality in the province. (He died in office. A big picture of Bernie hung in the hallway of the house. Nina and the girls would never leave the house without touching the picture and saying, "Bye, Daddy.") Annie ruled over the store and mothered all the neighbourhood children.

Mike Bowes, a former mayor himself and now a lawyer, remembered going to the store. Annie always grilled him. "She always wanted to know what you were doing. It was like an inquisition, but a kind one." Someone else remembered, "You went there for an ice cream and got a half hour of wisdom."

One of Annie's "children" said you were expected to pay her a call if you hadn't seen her for a while. "I remember one time I came home from somewhere and didn't stop in right away. A day or two later my sister said, 'Annie's been asking for you, you should drop by.' I forgot. The next night my sister came in from Annie's. 'For Jesus' sake, will you go over and visit Annie's,' she said. I dropped in a bit later, bought a quart of milk and talked for an hour."

Annie Flam was proud, tough, and kind – she would have a tea for one of the neighbourhood girl's first communion. "She was the most strong-willed woman on the Miramichi," said her cousin. And one of the most respected, said a former police chief.

Only once had she ever been afraid. In the 1970s, two young thugs robbed her store, shoving her against the freezer so hard that she hit her head. Flam kept a hatchet for protection after that, as well as a pair of scissors under her pillow. But they didn't help her the night of May 28, 1989.

Early next morning, a passerby noticed the fire. The house was so old the flames ripped through it. A policeman kicked in a back door on Bernie's side of the house.

Nina was lying at the bottom of the stairs, her nightie burned off. "Give me your coat, give me your coat," she kept saying. She had dragged herself down the stairs to escape the flames.

Only hours later, after what was left of the house had cooled, did they find Annie's body buried under the rubble. She was in her mother's bedroom, burned beyond recognition.

This was an arson. Police said later that the fire was set to cover up a robbery. But there was more. Nina, suffering from second- and third-degree burns, had been rushed to hospital in Fredericton, a two-hour drive away.

There police heard that she'd been sexually assaulted and badly beaten by a masked man. Police didn't release that information, however. Five months later a CBC reporter found out. By then, two more women had been sexually assaulted and beaten to death. The autopsy of Annie Flam showed that she too had been savagely beaten. Her jaw was broken. At first, police thought the intense heat from the fire had done that. But an anthropologist called in by police said no, only a severe blow could do that damage. This, too, police would keep to themselves.

Annie's funeral was held in Saint John. There, the rabbi led the mourners in praying the Kaddish, the Jewish prayer of life and death. Sam Rubenstein cried for his cousin, for her tragic death. And a young Irish Catholic cried for Annie, the woman who had given her tea on her first communion years before.

The investigation changed hands at the request of the provincial government. The RCMP took over from the

Chatham town police. Information on the investigation seemed to dry up. Neither the public nor the media knew what was going on.

Staff Sgt. Ben St. Onge, the bald and barrel-chested chief of the Newcastle RCMP detachment, disliked reporters. The feeling was mutual. St. Onge told a radio reporter that Allan Legere did not match the description of the killer given to police by Nina Flam. That seemed to rule him out. But not for long.

In the meantime, Sgt. Ernie Munden became the official RCMP media spokesman. A twenty-two-year veteran of the force, Munden would become the most familiar RCMP face on the Miramichi. He wasn't as imposing-looking as St. Onge, and he was much more approachable.

For his part, Munden said Legere hadn't been ruled out as a suspect, that he'd spoken to St. Onge and the evidence didn't show one way or the other that Legere was involved. Given Legere's record, he had to be considered a suspect. But even with Munden, openness with reporters was seemingly haphazard.

Regardless of what the police believed, the name of Allan Legere was on everyone's lips. People talked about the Glendenning murder. That was a store, too, they said. Everyone was agitated, staying awake at night.

At eleven-thirty on the night of June 1, a Chatham man drove into the driveway of his home in the Wellington Street area near Annie Flam's store. He spotted someone trying to break into a shed next to his house. The shed had been burglarized just before the Flam attack; a thief had dumped hockey gear out of a duffel bag and filled it with meat from a freezer. Now, it seemed, the thief, was back for more.

The homeowner hit the gas pedal, hurtling the car straight at the man, who turned and ran. It was close. The car went through a fence and stopped in a neighbour's yard. The thief scampered across the street and disappeared between two houses.

The next morning, a contractor on Wellington Street found a pair of eyeglasses in a hole dug for a sundeck. Police were cautious when they announced this discovery. Said Jack Bell, acting Chatham police chief: "These glasses were checked by an optometrist and are the same type, style, and prescription as worn by Allan Legere at the time of his escape from custody in Moncton."

The community wasn't quite so equivocal. Legere was still around. Period. Why, they didn't know.

At a press conference several days after the Wellington Street sighting, Munden warned people that the reality of trying to catch an escaped killer like Legere had little to do with the police shows people see on television. "It's very, very difficult to go ahead and locate somebody: a resident of the area who has in-depth knowledge of crimes, having committed crimes, who is very aware of the police situation.

"This is his home," he said of Legere. "He's quite comfortable in these surroundings." There could even be people helping him.

The Flam killing and the more than fifty sightings of Legere in the area set off a spree of security-system purchases. Some elderly people who could afford it had bars installed on basement windows. Hardware stores reported a sudden jump in the sales of deadbolts and door chains.

To make matters worse, two other convicts from the Miramichi were on the loose. Brothers David and John Tanasichuk had been serving time for break and enters, one in the Westmorland minimum-security institution at Dorchester, the other at a correctional facility in Parrsboro. On May 22, 1989, David had escaped. John followed soon after.

The Tanasichuks knew the Flams, and police considered David, along with Legere, a suspect in the murder of Annie.

At the same time, Crown prosecutor Fred Ferguson called the Tanasichuks "disorganized criminals." They were so inept that one of the brothers accidentally shot his partner while using a motorcycle to escape after a robbery. Still, they couldn't be discounted.

That is, until the RCMP found the Tanasichuk brothers an hour's drive south of Newcastle, near Harcourt. They'd been hiding at a hunting camp. After questioning them, police eliminated David as a murder suspect. The two were charged with being unlawfully at large.

The hunt for Legere continued. From time to time that summer intensive police manhunts were undertaken, using helicopter, dog teams, men on the ground. But nothing, absolutely nothing turned up. Police pressured Legere's friends. If they knew anything, they weren't talking.

Crime Stoppers offered a $2,000 reward for information leading to Legere's arrest. Again, no results.

A big manhunt in the Miramichi area occurred in mid-June when, acting on a tip, police with dogs and a helicopter combed woods around the Chatham industrial park. Again, nothing turned up. The next week sightings of Legere were reported in both Fredericton, more than 100 miles to the south, and the Caledon East area, northwest of Toronto.

Newcastle RCMP said they believed Legere was still nearby, but couldn't prove it. By July 25, though, they thought he might be gone. It was a feeling shared by many. After all, hadn't Legere been spotted shortly after his escape in the area where the emptied safe from the Glendenning home had been found in 1986? Everyone knew there were tens of thousands of dollars still missing from that robbery. It all seemed to fit.

"Unless he makes a mistake, they'll never find him," suggested the editor of the *Miramichi Leader*, Rick MacLean. "If the police couldn't catch him when they had him supposedly pinned down in woods near Moncton, and then when they had more than a dozen officers trying to track him down here in a community where everyone knows what he looks like, the odds are that unless he makes a mistake, he's gone for good."

It was a beautiful summer, and people were happy to try to forget what had happened.

Only a legal postscript remained. Legere had appealed his murder conviction to the Supreme Court of Canada. After his escape, the court announced that if he was still at large by the start of October, he would lose forever his chance for appeal. The decision to grant Legere extra time was highly unusual and prompted speculation that he had a good chance of getting the court to hear his case.

At the burned-out shell of Flam's grocery, a yellow police line kept people away. One day the line was gone. Later that summer, while Nina was recovering in hospital, her four daughters came to salvage whatever they could. They walked away without looking back.

A crane showed up and flattened the ruins. The rubbish was carted off. Now an empty lot is all that's left of Annie Flam's store.

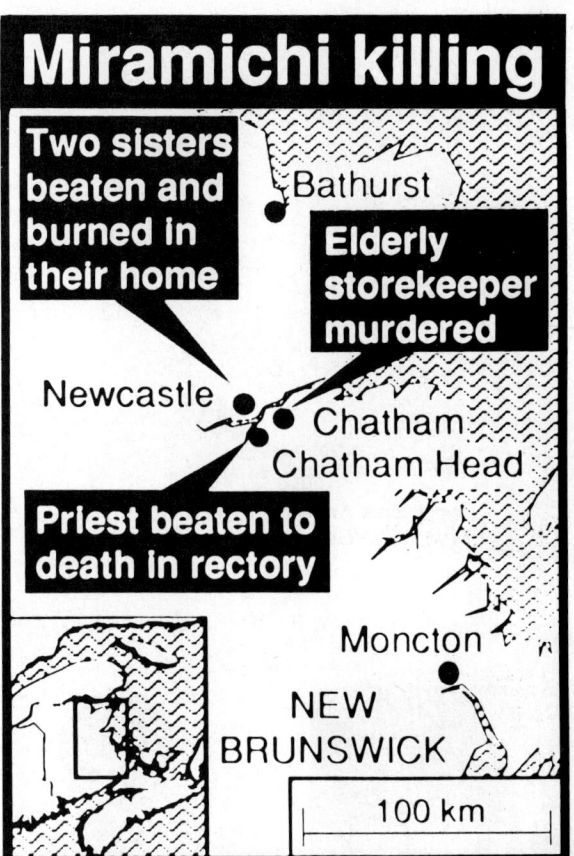

(Canapress)

Shopkeeper Annie Flam: murdered May, 1989. *(Guy Aube)*

Donna Daughney, 45, and her sister, Linda, 41: murdered October, 1989. *(Guy Aube)*

The death of Father James Smith, left, sent the Miramichi into a frenzy of panic. *(The Miramichi Leader)*

Police cordon off the Chatham Head rectory where the Catholic priest had lived. *(J.K.R. Walls)*

Priests of the Diocese of Saint John participate in the funeral of Father Smith. *(J.K.R. Walls)*

RCMP officers enter woods near Chatham to investigate a sighting of a man with a rifle Nov. 20.
(Canapress/Andrew Vaughan)

Police present a united front in one of several media conferences held during the seven-month terror.
(J.K.R. Walls)

Miramichi hunters are questioned by police and told to keep an eye out for any suspicious activity.
(J.K.R. Walls)

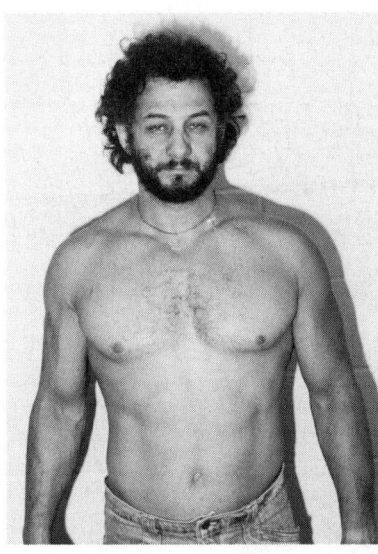

Allan Legere at the time of his arrest for the Glendenning murder in June, 1986.

Legere, second from left, as an elementary school pupil in the 1950s. *(J.K.R. Walls)*

Left: Legere at the time of his 1987 trial. *(J.K.R. Walls)*

Right: Legere in the 1970s. *(The Miramichi Leader)*

The gas station and convenience store at Sussex, N.B., where Legere spent some of his last, desperate moments of freedom. *(Kings County Record)*

Police investigators pore over the semi-trailer truck Legere hijacked the night of his capture. *(The Miramichi Leader/ Cathy Carnahan)*

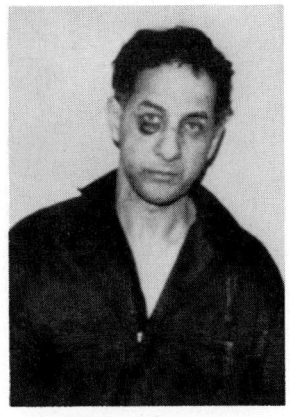

Allan Legere as he looked at the time of his capture Nov. 24, 1989. *(Canapress)*

Legere circa 1986. *(The Times-Transcript/Moncton)*

The police sketch of Legere – or a man investigators first thought was an accomplice – and the photo taken by police upon his capture. *(The Miramichi Leader/Willie Wark)*

Gas station clerk Joy Levesque *(Kings County Record)*

Crown prosecutor Fred Ferguson *(J.K.R. Walls)*

Trucker Brian Golding *(Willie Wark)*

RCMP Sgt. Ernest Munden *(J.K.R. Walls)*

NINE

Sudden Attacks

THE VIOLENCE returned just hours before the Supreme Court's deadline for Legere's appeal.

At abouty ten-thirty on Saturday night, September 30, Morrissy Doran of Newcastle picked up the phone to call the police. The seventy-year-old had been hit in the back by a blast from a shotgun. His attacker was a man about five feet, eleven inches tall with a medium to heavy build and dressed in what might have been a black leather jacket, dark clothing, and a ski mask. He had a light growth of beard.

The attacker had opened a basement window and crawled through. He came up the stairs into the house, demanding money. He got more than he bargained for. Doran fought back, but not successfully enough to avoid being wounded. His attacker took off. (Doran eventually recovered from his wounds.)

The next night, seventy-six-year-old Edwin (Sonny) Russell and his wife, Evangeline, sixty-three, were sitting in their home less than a five-minute walk from Doran's residence. At 9:20 they heard someone trying to get in through a basement window. The attacker got the window off, but then ran to the back door of the house. The man charged into the kitchen, a shotgun in hand.

Sonny wrestled with the assailant, driving the man out of the kitchen, into the yard and onto the street. The police station is thirty seconds away by car.

As had happened the night before, the attacker ran away when faced with a fight. This time he dropped his weapon.

Police had barely rushed to the Russell home when another call came in. Someone had tried to break into the home of Todd Matchett's father, Billy, about a two miles away on the south end of town. The Russells' attacker had run in that direction.

Police cars roared down the provincial highway that cuts Newcastle in half, arriving at Matchett's in minutes. A man matching the description of the attacker in the other two cases was spotted running away from the house.

A door-to-door search turned up nothing.

The investigation seemed to stall quickly, although police did say they were working on a good composite sketch of the man believed to have committed the attacks.

The incidents briefly rekindled the fear of the previous spring, but there were too many differences between the Flam murder and the assaults. The person responsible this time seemed an amateur compared to the person wanted for the Flam murder. While the elderly continued to take extra precautions, most of the community began to relax again rather quickly, confident that the person responsible for the latest violence would soon be caught.

A week later the story fell off the front pages of the local papers. The front page of the *Miramichi Leader* of October 11 featured stories about bilingualism, cutbacks at VIA Rail, and a short item mentioning that the Supreme Court of Canada was set to drop Legere's appeal case the next day.

A letter complaining about the willingness of Miramichi residents to accept the violence around them appeared in the weekend edition of the paper. Emily Vienneau of Newcastle blamed the sudden resurgence in the local economy, prompted by expansion of the pulp and paper mill, for much of the trouble. Undesirables were coming in and ruining the area's good name. "Have vigilante groups if that is what it takes," she wrote. "It's time the people woke up and died right, if they have to, instead of dying of fright."

It was Friday, October 13.

TEN

Two Sisters Living a Quiet Life

THE DAUGHNEY sisters, Linda and Donna, were happy. They'd be warm this winter. Their modest two-storey house, the house they'd lived in all their lives, was being insulated. The robin-egg blue siding would be on within a week.

Friday the thirteenth was one of the those beautiful warm fall days. Bernard Geikie was on his way to his camp. The fifty-six-year-old CN worker looked to his right and saw Donna in her back yard hanging up the wash. He waved at her, she at him.

They'd been neighbours for thirty-three years, ever since Bernard and Mary married. That was the way it was on Mitchell Street in Newcastle. You knew your neighbours, their children. It isn't as rich as many of the neighbourhoods in the town. This is working class and proud of it. They take care of their own.

"I can remember when they were both born," says Geikie of the Daughneys. "The street was being paved for the first time. I saw them grow up. When Donna graduated, she got dressed here to go to her prom."

Life wasn't easy for the Daughney daughters – Frances, Donna, and Linda – or their mother, Willa. Their father, Charlie, was an alcoholic. He didn't beat the girls, but he yelled at them often and sometimes locked them out of the house if they didn't come home when he said.

On Saturday mornings, Willa would walk the few steps to the Anderson saw mill, her children holding her hands. She would stand in line with the men, the only woman there, waiting for Charlie's cheque. If she didn't get it before he did, he would spend it on a drinking binge, leaving nothing for his family to live on until the next Saturday.

Those painful memories marked the children for the rest of their lives. "Donna didn't talk about her childhood much. But she was bitter about it," said a girlfriend.

Frances moved away, eventually settling in Alaska. For a time, Donna went to work in Ontario. She returned to the Miramichi after her mother died to take care of her father and sister. When Charlie died, the sisters were alone.

Linda, forty-one, was shy. Donna, four years older, looked out for her. A girlfriend remembered a group of them going to the Legion. "Donna was very protective of Linda. Linda wasn't slow or retarded as some people said, just extremely timid, to the point of being frightened if someone asked her to dance. If Donna thought someone was bothering her younger sister, she could be fiercely protective, to the point of telling men to get lost."

Said Geikie, "Donna would light up your room when she walked in. If it was a dull day, she'd light it up."

She was in good shape, walked about eight miles a

day, and used to work out in the same gym as Allan Legere. Did they ever meet? No one knows for sure, but Donna's girlfriend said, "Rumours that Linda or Donna might have gone out with Legere are nonsense. Linda was so shy she would have run if someone had asked her out, and Donna wasn't the kind to have anything to do with someone like Legere."

Neither had a boyfriend. Donna used to have one, but that involvement ended unhappily. She'd tell friends that she never wanted to marry, that she didn't want a husband to treat her like her father had treated her mother and them.

Linda didn't work; a skin condition, eczema, prevented that. She received a small pension. Donna worked part-time for the Department of Income Assistance, the welfare department.

The sisters had a routine that never changed in all the time they were at home. They ate supper at 4:30, and at 5:10 Linda walked the hundred feet to the Geikies for tea. The Geikies were the only "family" the girls had left. "We considered them our daughters. You couldn't have girls come into your house every day and have the relationship they had with my children and grandchildren and not think that way."

October 13 seemed to come and go like any other day. Donna put her clothes on the line. Linda dropped by for tea. Later that night, Linda and a friend walked to a nearby Tim Horton's franchise for coffee and doughnuts, then headed home around eleven o'clock. They returned to the friend's apartment just a few hundred feet from the sisters' home. Linda left, forgetting her gloves. The friend tried to get her attention but failed. Oh well, she thought, I'll give them to her in the morning.

Early Saturday, a volunteer firefighter saw smoke coming from an upstairs window on Mitchell Street. He ran around the corner to the fire station.

The first firefighters to arrive at the Daughney residence rushed in without oxygen masks. Battling smoke and heat, they managed to find the sisters upstairs, in the same bedroom. Donna was in her bed, Linda was on the floor.

They extinguished the blaze before it could spread to the ground floor. But what the firefighters saw in the bedroom could mean only one thing. Arson and murder.

Word spread quickly and so did the fear, the shock, the numbness, the realization that perhaps a serial killer was on the loose, preying on the old and the helpless. It was just like the Flams, people said. A fire set to cover a robbery. A robbery done to cover a murder.

Both women had been sexually assaulted. Donna had been beaten to death. Linda had been beaten too, but the actual cause of her death was smoke inhalation. Although police weren't saying, there was speculation that Linda may have walked right into the attacker's grasp. Only one thing could be certain, a family friend said weeks later – Donna Daughney would have fought.

"I remember her saying she'd die before she'd let anything happen to Linda," the friend said. "She would fight until there was no fight left in her body to protect her. She would have died rather than let Linda walk into that, that night. She must have been dead or dying."

News of the attack sent a chill through nextdoor neighbour Mrs. Jim Murray. She had heard something that night after eleven. It sounded like someone kicking a ladder. She looked out, but saw nothing. "If I had turned on the back light, maybe I might have seen. It just gives you the creeps."

"This is not supposed to go on in our little province, our little town, our little Miramichi," Bernard Geikie said later, fighting the tears, unconsciously folding and unfolding the glasses in his hands. "They were just two beautiful people. Nobody had a bad word for them."

Everyone who knew the Daughneys said the same thing. "Just nice people," said the coroner. "There's no reason at all for this. Somebody's sick," added the funeral director.

Word spread, too, of two incidents committed the same night as the murders. A Chatham businessman living in a residential part of Newcastle was watching cable television with his wife when the picture suddenly went fuzzy. The man heard a noise outside and when he turned on the back light he saw someone running away. The cable wire to the house, it turned out, had been cut. Possibly, it had been mistaken for a telephone line.

At midnight at a home just minutes from the Daughney house, Gary Forrest and his girlfriend were downstairs in his mother's home when they heard a crash. Gary climbed the stairs, thinking something had happened to his mother. Instead, he spotted a thief jumping out a window, taking money and jewellery with him.

Suddenly there seemed to be more Mounted Police on the Miramichi. They were looking for Allan Legere – and a killer. Maybe they were one and the same, maybe they weren't. But the pressure to do something, anything, before the situation got any worse was intense.

Still, if the RCMP were getting anywhere, they weren't saying so publicly.

The first police news release after the Daughney

deaths said little other than who the women were and that they had been beaten. There was also this discomforting paragraph: "The public is aware of a recent rash of violent crime in the Miramichi region. Police are examining these incidents and evidence to determine if they are linked and perpetrated by the same individual."

(There were arguments between senior RCMP staff in Fredericton and officers in Newcastle over what to release after the murders. Senior staff wanted only the bare minimum out. It was a decision that would backfire.)

If there were suddenly more police, there were also more reporters and more television crews, and not just from New Brunswick. Three possibly related murders and an escaped convicted killer made for a powerful story. This wasn't *Murder She Wrote* and Angela Lansbury wasn't going to solve the mystery in the next sixty minutes. This was real, and no one knew who would be the next victim.

Miramichiers were resentful of the attention. Their lives, their troubles, were under a media microscope. They were scared, on edge, and having microphones and cameras shoved at them didn't help. The killer might see their faces. Why chance it?

Three days after the murders, Sgt. Ernie Munden spoke with a group of reporters in the small coffee room of the Newcastle detachment. He said there were similarities between the Flam murder and the Daughney murders, but they weren't conclusive proof. Yes, there might be a serial killer out there, but that had to be determined. Yes, Legere was a suspect "due to his conviction for a similar crime of violence, being unlawfully at large and having resided in the community," but he wasn't the only suspect.

"If Legere is responsible," Munden said, "he must be apprehended. If he is not, it is important not to mislead people into thinking he is the prime suspect."

He asked for the public's help, even the help of criminals in the area. "The criminal community has its own code of ethics and would not and should not tolerate this and previous crimes." Someone, he said, was helping and hiding this killer.

He pleaded with people not to buy or use guns for protection – a plea that went unheeded. People were too scared to listen.

Though Munden wasn't involved in the day-to-day investigation of the murders, he had seen what the killer had done. It unnerved him, shook him up as a policeman, a parent, and a religious man. His control, the carefully modulated voice, broke as the news conference wrapped up. Picking up the photographs of Donna and Linda Daughney, he said: "I've only seen these people in the hospital, in the morgue. It is very difficult to see the loss of human life, especially when it comes to women, even more so, children. The person or persons who took their lives has to be brought to justice very, very quickly. It is a terrible crime."

There were tears in his eyes.

Wednesday's weather, cold and raw, foreshadowed the coming winter. At one o'clock, one hundred and fifty people walked and drove up the short, steep hill leading to the St. James and St. John United Church in Newcastle for the joint funeral. The sisters were Anglican, but their own church was too small for the turnout of Miramichiers.

It was a short service. The choir sang "The Lord is My Shepherd" and "How Firm a Foundation." Father Barry Thorley, told the congregation to keep their faith in God, not to lose hope, in spite of the murders. "It is not our town nor the community around this town that is wicked and evil. Rather it is a presence within the town, and consequently amongst us, which is based on evilness and wickedness."

The pallbearers led the two caskets out of the church. Frances, the only living sister, stood up and tried to touch the coffins, but her husband and Bernard Geikie gently held her back.

Then the procession went to the cemetery to bury Donna and Linda Daughney – "two nice people." They'd had a hard life, a harder death.

ELEVEN

I've Got a Secret

ON OCTOBER 17, the Liberal MP for Moncton, George Rideout pleaded in the House of Commons for more help for the RCMP working on the Miramichi murders. He described the people of the region as being in a state of panic. "These crimes are most violent and heinous," he said. "On the basis of information that I have been given, the RCMP is short-staffed in New Brunswick due in part to the new peacekeeping role." (Five RCMP officers from the province were in Namibia, Africa, helping police the election there. None were from Newcastle, although one was from the French community of Rogersville about twenty-five miles to the southeast.)

"I am further advised that some members of the force who have an intimate knowledge of Newcastle have not been utilized. Would the minister [Solicitor General Pierre Blais] commit the additional staff necessary so a full, complete and expeditious investigation can be carried out immediately?"

Meanwhile, New Brunswick RCMP concentrated on keeping a tight lid on any information related to the double killing. The same day that Rideout spoke in Ottawa, Sgt. Ernie Munden told reporters that no composite drawing of a suspect would be released. Doing so might hurt the investigation by giving the attacker a chance to change his appearance, he explained. He repeated that the Daughney sisters had been sexually assaulted and brutally beaten, but added that, to protect the investigation and the family, no further details on the attack would be released.

At the same time, he stressed the need for help from the public. "We can't solve a crime solely by ourselves."

The public, for its part, was reacting from its collective gut. People desperately looked for ways to protect themselves. The provincial utilities company, N.B. Power, added three extra crews to try to keep up with the jump in demand for dusk-to-dawn lights. Staff ordered an additional two hundred lights to be installed in people's yards and on dark sections of local streets. Crews put up as many as fifteen a day. They might have done more, but they could work only during daylight hours because people refused to answer their doors after dark.

Individuals selling dogs were inundated with calls. Town officials had to assure organizers of a meeting of a thousand teachers set for Newcastle that the area was still safe to visit. Scanners capable of picking up police broadcasts disappeared from stores as fast as they came in. One man ended up buying a unit worth more than $200 in Yarmouth, Nova Scotia – hundreds of miles away – and having it delivered by visiting relatives. Communities cancelled Halloween trick-or-treating, fearing the killer might use the chance to strike again. Parties for children were organized in town and village halls instead. Police warned all would-be trick-or-treaters that anyone found walking the streets wearing a mask would be taken in for questioning.

The Moncton-based Creative Security Systems decided to expand into the Miramichi area three weeks earlier than planned because of the potential business. The home-safety business even increased in Moncton, about ninety miles away. In high demand was a remote panic-button system capable of setting off an alarm at the police station.

In Newcastle, people living near the Daughney home set up their own version of a security system. "Every door and window is secure," explained Edith Russell, an elderly woman who worked as a crosswalk guard at a local school. "And I've told my neighbours what to do if they need my help. All they have to do is bang on the wall and I will be able to hear them. My neighbours across the street have my telephone number. Also, if they come outside and yell, I will be able to hear them."

Yet even these precautions offered little comfort in the face of such senseless violence. "They don't want money, it seems, they just want to beat and kill," Russell said. "It's just terrible. Everyone is so scared and nervous. They're all old people on this street. The Daughneys were the youngest ones living here. You have to think of everything. Nina Flam's brother lives on this street, right across from where the girls were murdered. Maybe whoever did this to them mistook the house for his."

Russell quickly became something of a media star because she was one of the few people willing to talk, appearing on CBC Radio's national program "As It Happens" and CBC TV's "The Journal." (Soon, though, even

Russell stopped talking. A few weeks later, when "The Journal" tried to get her back on the show, the program was told that her family wouldn't allow it.)

On October 18, just hours after the Daughneys were buried, about three hundred people crammed into the main auditorium of the Newcastle town hall for a public forum organized by CBC Radio Moncton. The plan was to talk about what people could do to cope with the violence. The auditorium crowd had another idea, however. Angry at the police for not yet catching whoever was responsible, upset at the scant bits of information released so far, they wasted little time in getting to the point.

If the man who committed these murders came into his home and threatened his wife and infant son, said Gordie Graham of Newcastle, the police would have to carry the man out feet first. Applause swept through the hall.

"There's not a jury in the world that's going to convict you for shooting scum like that," another man said, to more cheers.

Munden pleaded with people not to take the law into their hands. A homeowner must be prepared to defend his or her actions the same way a police officer must. If a thief is shot during a robbery, the homeowner could face criminal charges, he warned.

Munden's pleas met with little enthusiasm. People cheered when a man stood up and said that his home is his castle. He'd do what he had to do to protect it.

"What's a person supposed to do?" another shouted. "Wait for an attacker to come in and shoot him?"

Senior citizen Don Whalen, a member of the panel set up for the meeting, complained about the lack of information coming out and the effect it was having on the elderly. "There's no information, none whatsoever to satisfy and cool the feelings down so that at least we know that someone is out there working for their interests. The police are keeping everything to themselves."

Few people went to the microphones to speak during the meeting. Said one woman afterwards: "More of us wanted to get up and say something, but we were too scared with the TV cameras there."

The next day, Newcastle town council voted to give $10,000 to the Crime Stoppers special fund aimed at ending the crime wave. Within twenty-four hours, the fund shot past the $25,000 goal, nearing the $30,000 mark.

Later that day, Newcastle town police at last released a sketch of the suspect in the attacks three weeks earlier on Morrissy Doran and the Russells. The drawing showed a heavy-set man with a stubble of beard and dark, curly hair. Everyone in the area immediately saw resemblances to people they knew. Long-time residents with no record of causing trouble suddenly had dangerous pasts and kinky habits. Calls flooded police lines. One local shopowner became the subject of so many rumours that he had to go to the *Miramichi Leader* to refute them. Some people mistakenly thought the sketch was that of the man who killed the Daughney sisters and Annie Flam.

A TV story calling the Miramichi a "little Detroit" prompted Newcastle councillor Rick Matthews to spring to his town's defence. "We have a bad situation and everyone is fearful, but Newcastle certainly can't be compared to a small Detroit," he said. "People still walk our streets in Newcastle, but with great concern."

Criticism of the police began to appear in print. A reader wrote to the *Miramichi Leader*: "I am afraid our local police, often called Canada's finest, are doing a terrible job. Annie Flam is dead and buried, yet little has been done. I am afraid this last double murder will go the same route. I am sick of hearing how good the RCMP are. Let's have a demonstration to prove it so my family and I can relax in our home."

At a news conference on October 27, Munden decided to announce that police had no evidence linking Legere to the Daughney killings. It looked as though the often stormy relationship between the RCMP and the media was improving. Munden answered a range of questions. Calling in a psychic would be a last resort, and no, there was no evidence that this was a cult killing. No, there was no description as yet of the attacker in the Flam case.

The thaw proved short-lived. A terse news release issued soon after by the RCMP headquarters in Fredericton told reporters not to expect any more news conferences. Further information would come only in a news release "upon receipt of information and in a written format." Why? To ensure consistency in the information provided to the public, police said.

The timing of the crackdown could hardly have been worse. At eleven o'clock on the night of Saturday, October 28, Const. Robert Bruce of the Chatham police department heard a shot in downtown Chatham. About the same time, a man broke into a truck parked next to the Morada Motel, up the street from the town hall. He stole two guns and fled across town on foot. Town police and the RCMP sealed off the area but came up empty.

Two hours later, on the other end of town, a man was watching television. San Francisco and Oakland were battling it out in the World Series. The man headed to the kitchen for a drink of water. He noticed a figure in the yard and stepped outside to investigate.

"Get back inside," snarled a man, a gun at the ready.

The homeowner ran inside, shut off the lights, and hit the floor. Then he crawled to the phone and called the police.

Outside, the man with the gun coolly smashed a window of a car in the driveway and tore through the glove compartment. Nothing was taken. (The next day it was discovered that the home once belonged to a member of the 1987 jury that convicted Allan Legere of murder. The man had since moved but was still living on the Miramichi. Police refused to say if the strange visit in the middle of a chase was significant.)

There was more to come that Saturday. Police brought in a dog, which immediately picked up a fresh scent and headed down the hill to the river. The chase continued for more than a mile south, in the direction of Chatham Head. The man ran along some railway tracks circling behind the Miramichi Golf and Country Club. Suddenly he wheeled and shot at the RCMP officer with the dog. Police held their fire. The man then disappeared.

By two in the morning, more RCMP were being brought in and roads leading out of the area sealed off. Homes were evacuated, other people were told to stay inside with the doors locked. One resident later reported that he saw a group of police officers in his front yard and a man with a gun out back near the woods. The homeowner mistook the man for another officer and waved. The man spun around and dashed into the woods.

Police continued to press the search, giving up

shortly before noon Sunday. They would be back. Monday morning, a woman looked out her window to see two police officers in fatigues roar by in a Jeep. Their faces were blackened and they carried special eyewear, probably glasses to enhance night vision.

Around the same time as the Chatham incidents, people with small camps in the woods about twenty miles south of the area started reporting strange happenings. One man said he had entered his camp about two weeks earlier and found that someone had helped himself to a meal. A plate, knife, and fork were used, then left neatly arranged. Another said that a few hours before the chase Saturday night he spotted a car – either a Lincoln or Marquis – near the road leading to his camp. The car sped away when spotted. It happened a couple of times that day, the man said.

By Monday, telephone lines were abuzz as reporters and a public frantic for more information tried to figure out what the RCMP were doing. The police weren't just refusing to answer questions; they wouldn't even come to the phone.

An RCMP handout revealed almost nothing: "On Saturday, Oct. 28, 1989, at approximately 1107 hours, the R.C.M. Police Newcastle Detachment, responded to a request for assistance from the Chatham Police Detachment. The Chatham Police were investigating a prowler complaint; complaint of a discharged firearm and a male being observed with a weapon. The investigation continued from a westerly area outside the Chatham Town limits to Morrison Cove and the Miramichi Golf and Country Club area, concluding at 11:35 A.M. Additional resources, including members of neighboring detachments were utilized, coupled with specialized units already available. Both the Chatham Police and R.C.M.

Police are continuing their respective investigations. No further comments or details are being provided due to the ongoing investigation."

The terseness of the release irritated many. *Miramichi Leader* editor Rick MacLean took shots at the RCMP both in a television interview aired Tuesday night on ATV – the CTV affiliate in Maritime provinces – and the next day in a lead editorial. He hit hard at the police for refusing to answer any questions about what had gone on in the back yards in Chatham.

"The RCMP have reverted to their old ways." MacLean wrote. "The force has asked for help from the public in solving the recent series of crimes in the area. But they seem to think they will get the help they need without providing anything meaningful in the way of information to the public."

The entire RCMP statement was quoted to show people how little information was being given out. This was followed by a list of things the community wanted to know: "Do they have any suspects? Has anyone been questioned? Is there some sort of description of the person sought? Male, female? Black, white? Was anyone hurt? We know shots were fired at an officer of the RCMP. There's not a mention of that. We know a chopper was called in. Nothing about that either.

"People are afraid it might be the escaped killer Allan Legere," the editorial continued. "There's nothing mentioned one way or the other. And no one from the detachment will answer any questions, so we'll not find out anything else from them. If this is the RCMP's idea of how the people of the Miramichi should be treated, then the RCMP has fallen off the deep end when it comes to common sense.

"We're *eager* to help. *Desperate* to help. We're

frightened and we want this to end. Yet the RCMP feels it should treat us like children who deserve only to be seen, but not heard. Such treatment is outrageous. Either that, or this province should rethink the idea of setting up its own force – one that is more sensitive to the concerns of the people it is paid to serve and protect."

The editorial and TV interview prompted a visit the next day from RCMP Supt. Al Rivard of Moncton, the officer in charge of the overall investigation. The news blackout by the RCMP had been the result of a misunderstanding, Rivard said. He had meant for Sgt. Ernie Munden to respond to calls but not to go before the cameras unless there was something new to report. He was also concerned about talk that the police forces might not be co-operating with each other. He insisted they were.

Rivard confirmed that the RCMP were about to set up a special major crime unit in an unused provincial government building near Chatham. He also said that there were about eighty police officers in the area ready to help if needed. That included the various local police forces and twenty-six members of the RCMP detachment in Newcastle.

The visit marked a sudden improvement in relations between the media and the RCMP, but *Miramichi Leader* publisher David Cadogan was still angry at what he saw as a long-standing problem. He let fly with a column in the Friday edition of the paper, naming names as he went.

"The RCMP are nationally renowned for their arrogant and ignorant treatment of the public with regard to information about their activities," he wrote.

"Local RCMP commander Ben St. Onge is the worst example of the old, unaccountable thinking I've seen in a career of dealing with the RCMP. He has, at times, actually seemed to enjoy frustrating the efforts of the media to do a proper job. His behavior after the Flam murder had media representatives from far and wide burning up the wires with complaints.

"The situation improved somewhat with the appointment of Ernie Munden to the investigation and as spokesman. Unfortunately, the curtain was brought down again earlier this week. Again the public was left with so little information that the wildest rumors have as much credibility as fact. The public wants to help. It is hard to do that without any information except a rough description in a sketch. Even that was withheld from the public for quite some time.

"There must be some information we could have that would help us narrow down what we're all thinking about," Cadogan said. "Rumor has it that the attacker of Nina Flam and Morrissy Doran and the Russells spoke to them. Did he sound local? Did he have local knowledge or personal knowledge of his victims? Did he have an accent or local flavor to his speech? Is there forensic evidence to connect these crimes? Give us some clues and perhaps we'll be able to watch, notice, remember and think more usefully."

He found the attitude of the RCMP mystifying. "On the one hand, the police work hand in hand with Crime Stoppers . . . . On the other hand, the RCMP plays 'I've got a secret' with the most horrible series of crimes we can remember. What is going on? Are we waiting for this to come out on video?"

The various local police forces banded together later that day to try to display their solidarity and to attempt to defuse the mounting criticism. At a news conference, police chiefs Jack Bell of Chatham and Dan Newton of Newcastle joined Rivard and Munden.

Complaints about a lack of information, Munden charged, weren't coming from the public. "I think criticism is being directed through the media. Whether it is a co-ordinated response, or by some member of the media, I don't know."

A great deal of work had been done, the RCMP told reporters. More than fifty suspects had been interviewed and their alibis checked. Annual leaves for officers had been cancelled.

Cadogan's warning about a lack of information opening the door to wild rumours proved timely, as word was spreading that the Daughney sisters had been killed by a member of a cult who tore out their eyes, broke their legs and slashed their faces.

On November 9, the RCMP debunked the tale. Said Munden, "Donna and Linda Daughney sustained severe injuries in the facial area and elsewhere, the result of a severe beating. They were sexually assaulted. The bodies were not mutilated. There is no evidence of a Satanic cult."

The RCMP also said that no further information would be released until the next Wednesday, November 15. But those plans changed over the weekend, when the RCMP announced what everyone had believed all along: it appeared the Flam and Daughney cases were the work of the same person. Something had turned up in lab tests performed in Ottawa, but they wouldn't say what. The police did say in the same news release that "Allan Legere continues to be a suspect in this murder investigation and a warrant continues to be held by the Moncton police department for his escape from lawful custody."

It was an artfully worded statement. Legere was not

described as the prime suspect in the killings, but his was the only name mentioned in connection with the case. Reporters were invited to read between the lines. Some officers had wanted the release to go all the way and name Legere, but the decision was made to try the more subtle approach. The attempt failed. Reporters weren't ready to make the leap. The RCMP would have to do it.

On Monday, November 13, CBC TV's André Veniot reported police had indeed found something in their lab tests to identify Allan Legere as the prime suspect. Hair, semen, or both were involved in the tests. The key to the police's conclusion was a new technique called genetic fingerprinting, which matched the genetic make-up of material culled during the police investigation to samples of material taken from Legere.

The fight to get the necessary laboratory work done had taken months. Some officers had been convinced from the start that Legere had to be considered the prime suspect in the Flam killing. They lobbied unsuccessfully for genetic fingerprinting work to be done immediately. But the Canadian lab wouldn't be ready in the summer of 1989, the officers were told. They would have to wait until it was, and that wouldn't be until sometime in 1990.

But things changed after the Daughney killings. Now the agony of the Miramichi was on "The National" and "Canada AM." Front-page stories were appearing on newspapers across the country. Just as suddenly, the lab was able to do the work, and quickly. The results confirmed suspicions and intuitions.

The *Miramichi Leader*'s MacLean and CBC TV's Veniot broke the story a day ahead of a police news conference scheduled to announce it. The news was the talk of the province for about sixty minutes – until 7:05 P.M., November 16.

That's when parishioners peeked through the kitchen window of the rectory of a Roman Catholic priest in Chatham Head. There was blood everywhere.

TWELVE

Safe in the House of God

As A BOY growing up in Lower Newcastle in the Dirty Thirties, James V. Smith was skinny and tall. In a world that loved to hang a nickname on someone – one of the local boxers was called Clyne "Hopalong" Cassidy after the movie star – it was natural he would be called Slim Jim.

The Smiths were a big family, with nine children. "Slim" Jim was the third, and the brains of the family.

"He was more the student type. He'd read something once and remember it," recalled his older brother Leonard. The closest to Jim in age and friendship, Leonard watched his brother skip Grade 7 and end up in his class, much to his childhood embarrassment. They attended a one-room schoolhouse, so he only had to move over a few desks.

Jim won every prize when he graduated from high school, but he had his eyes on a bigger prize, one he never talked about much with his brother or, apparently, anyone else in his family.

"There was a big storm the summer before college," Leonard remembered. "The streets of Newcastle were covered with pulpwood, pine trees were broken. We were walking along and he told me he was going to become a priest." He was ordained May 6, 1945. Slim Jim became Father Jim.

Smith loved photography and travelling. He visited the Holy Land four times, Rome six times, and had been around the world. To save money on his last trip to the Middle East he went as a guide.

He was known to be a good man with a dollar, earning a reputation as a smart administrator, a priest who could turn around a parish in financial trouble. That's what he did in Chatham Head. At the time of his appointment in the late 1960s, the parish couldn't afford to pay the interest on its mortgage.

But slowly, with hard work, and Father Smith leading the way, the parish paid off the mortgage, replaced the oil furnace with electric heat in the Nativity of the Blessed Virgin Mary Church, and put siding on the building and on the rectory.

If Father Jim could cut a deal that saved the parish money, so much the better. He once walked up to the counter of a Zeller's store to pay for a popcorn popper. When he asked for a church discount, the clerk asked if he might provide a letter for their records to explain the lower price. Father Jim smiled his dry smile, pointed to his clerical collar, and said, "Isn't this good enough?"

Besides his fiscal skills, it was his camera everyone seems to remember. He was always using it, taking pictures at school, graduations, skating parties.

"I remember him going to take our picture when we were in Grade 11," says Jane, a middle-aged woman now. "We were acting the gawk" (local slang for fooling around).

"'Okay', he said, 'if you don't want your picture taken, then . . . '

"'No, no Father,' we said. 'We'll behave.'

"In those days, you were brought up to stand and listen every time a priest or nun walked into a room."

Father Jim also doubled as an archivist. He saved photographs, and boxed and catalogued them. Jane recalled the time some students were planning a high school reunion and wanted photos to put on a wall. "We called him and he said come over. When we got there, he had all the boxes out, with the years labelled on them. We were looking through and I remember saying, 'Look at that, that was in Grade 7.' 'No,' he corrected me. 'That was in Grade 6.' And it was."

In the early 1980s Father Smith had a heart attack, just before he and Leonard were to embark on a cruise. But it didn't really slow him down. By the time 1989 rolled around, Father Smith was sixty-nine and certainly eligible for retirement, yet he chose to continue to serve the parish.

The priest maintained the family home in Lower Newcastle and would retreat there when he could, enjoying walks along its sandy beach by the Miramichi. Once asked if the priesthood was a lonely life, he replied that it was sometimes, but sometimes he enjoyed that loneliness.

Every year he organized a cookout for the choir. The summer of 1989 was no different, even though it was a more difficult summer than most. His sister Alice, a nun, had died of cancer in July.

Smith wasn't one to be stampeded into changing his life, despite the months of murder and fear in the region. "He never appeared frightened or worried by it or to think he was in danger," Leonard said. In fact, the brothers were planning a trip to Hawaii, even though Father Jim had just returned from an excursion to Korea.

Throughout the summer and fall of 1989, he encouraged his parishioners to stay calm, to keep their faith. The killing and terror would pass, he predicted.

Jane bumped into him a few days before his death. "We talked about the escape of Allan Legere and all the killings that had gone on. He wasn't afraid. I said to him, 'Father, why don't you move out of that rectory until this is over? You could move into the rectory here in Chatham.'

"He had this funny way of holding his hands behind his back. Then he'd start rocking on his heels and lick his lips, as if pausing to think. 'Oh no,' he said. 'How would it look to my parishioners, me leaving and them having to stay in their homes?'"

He could stay at the church during the day and go to the Chatham rectory at night, Jane suggested. Although the house was on the main road, surrounded by other homes, there was a small stand of trees on one side, and Father Smith was alone at the rectory, without a resident housekeeper. Her suggestion fell on deaf ears. "'Oh, I don't think he's looking for God,' he said to me. 'He'll not come where God is.'"

On Thursday evening, November 16, about thirty parishioners were waiting for mass to begin in the Nativity of the Blessed Virgin Mary Church. Father Smith hadn't been seen that day, but it didn't matter; he was a punctual man and would be there for seven o'clock mass.

It didn't happen this time. Two parishioners ventured

to the back of the church, but Father Smith wasn't there. At 7:05 they headed next door to the rectory. They opened the door leading into the kitchen, and saw blood, blood everywhere.

They staggered back, horrified. Someone called the police. Parishioners clutched their rosaries and began saying Hail Marys.

"All of us were praying Father Smith would be all right," recalled Irene Roach, former president of the Catholic Women's League and a woman who knew the priest well. "But we knew in our hearts he wouldn't be. Everyone was crying, even the men."

The police arrived quickly. By now, they had a two-minute response time to any call. Roadblocks were set up throughout the area. RCMP officers with pump-action shotguns examined every car.

At the rectory, even veteran police officers weren't prepared for what they saw. Police refused to release details, but one veteran said later that it was the worst attack he'd seen in his career. True to the pattern, the violence was getting worse with each attack.

Father Smith had been savagely beaten. It may have taken a long time for him to die. His killer could have been hiding in the house for some time, perhaps nearly a day, keeping the priest captive. One RCMP officer said later that, as he stood outside in the church parking lot and thought of what was inside, he felt as if he had been shot in the guts. Somehow, he thought, we've failed.

A priest from a neighbouring parish came to give his brother in Christ the last rites.

That evening the news of Father Smith's death spread quickly. Phone circuits jammed, prompting police to issue a radio and television appeal asking people to stop using their phones because officers were having difficulty taking and receiving calls.

Fear became hysteria. Everyone seemed to think the same thing: he's killed a priest, no one is safe.

For once, police were not stingy with information. Within hours they had released a two-page detailed report on what they had discovered. They needed the public's help and knew it.

Someone had noticed some unusual activity around six-thirty that night. The horn of a car in the rectory garage began to blare. And shortly before seven, another witness saw Father Smith's 1984 Oldsmobile Delta 88 leave the garage and head towards Chatham. The priest wasn't at the wheel; someone with long, dark hair was.

The car, with a broken window on the driver's side, was found at ten that night at a motel in Bathurst, fifty miles to the northeast, near the train station.

The RCMP checked the VIA train schedule. A train had left Bathurst for Montreal only an hour before. They called Quebec Provincial Police for help. During the train stop at Levis, just across the St. Lawrence River from Quebec City, QPP officers boarded the train, and talked to passengers. They were told to look out for Legere, who had a distinctive tattoo on his right forearm. According to a June 5, 1989, wanted poster issued by the RCMP, the tattoo was an eagle's head and a star.

The QPP looked at the right arm of a passenger calling himself Ferdinand Savoie. He had "007" tattooed on one arm, but no eagle. However, they failed to check Savoie's left arm. What the officers didn't know was that the description on the wanted poster was accurate except for one crucial detail: the tattoo of the eagle head and star was on Legere's *left* arm, not his right.

The dawning of Friday didn't make living on the Miramichi any easier. There was a killer, perhaps more than one, on the loose and police didn't have him.

In Chatham Head, part of the church's large parking lot was roped off with yellow police ribbon. People in houses next to the church peered out windows, trying to find out what was going on. White-and-blue RCMP cruisers were everywhere. An RCMP dogmaster with a German shepherd combed the grounds of the rectory. A red wooden ladder, stolen from a neighbour and possibly used to enter the rectory, remained propped against the garage wall. Inside, the safe stood open, leading some to suggest robbery as a motive.

The curious stood on the steps of the senior citizens' home across the street, the home where Father Smith had been on the board of directors and visited all the time, just as he always visited the sick in the hospital. (The home has since been named Father Smith Manor.)

Cars pulled over just to look, others drove slowly by. "I almost had two accidents so far today from staring at the other drivers," one woman told a reporter. "Everybody looks like Allan Legere today."

People's anger boiled over onto the RCMP. When someone asked when police first got to the rectory, a man shot back, "Too fucking late, that's when."

That afternoon Superintendent Rivard and Sergeant Munden told reporters that they believed Legere had an accomplice – a tall, thin man. They confirmed that Legere was the prime suspect in the murders of the three women as well as a suspect in Father Smith's death.

They warned any friends of Legere's to give him up. "A word of caution to friends and associates of Legere. Allan Legere is considered one of the most dangerous and wanted criminals in Canada," Munden said.

And why was Legere back on the Miramichi? "He said he would come back to the community and make the community pay. He has voiced that he would go ahead and seek retribution from the community," Munden warned. "Everyone is a potential victim."

The price on Legere's head went higher still. Munden said the Crime Stoppers reward was now $50,000 for any information leading to his arrest and another $50,000 for information that would help end the crime wave on the Miramichi.

Rivard and Munden bristled when asked about bringing in the army to help in the search. Already more than a hundred police were looking for Legere. "I don't need more people," said Rivard. "What I need is more information."

The provincial government concurred. Rivard could have as many officers as he needed, as much money as he needed. "Money is no problem. This is more important than money," said the Solicitor General Conrad Landry.

A few days later, Premier Frank McKenna, as the MLA for Chatham, decided to return home to be with the people of his riding. He would stay with friends and run the government from Chatham, while his family would stay in Fredericton. "It's time," he declared, "to join together to share with our neighbours the pain we are all feeling and to provide better security for each other."

The premier announced that more RCMP officers were coming to join the investigation, prompting some to ask why these officers were needed now when police earlier had said that they had plenty of men.

Besides more police, McKenna promised a 911 number would be set up on the Miramichi, and money found to establish Neighbourbood Watch programs.

Solving this case was the most important "issue" in the province, he said. While some accused the premier of grandstanding, the *Times and Transcript* in Moncton, for one, praised the Liberal leader for his action, calling it the right thing to do at the right time.

That Friday night, one day after Father Smith's body was found, more than a thousand people gathered in St. Mary's Roman Catholic Church in Newcastle for a prayer service. Bishop Edward Troy of Saint John said that Father Smith's fellow priests remembered his gentleness and kindness and asked people not to give in to the anger and frustration they felt, but to turn it into prayer.

On Sunday, about a thousand persons visited the funeral home in Chatham for the wake. On Monday, Father Smith's parishioners gathered in his own church to pray for him and for themselves.

Snow fell heavily on the region on Tuesday, November 21, yet mourners filled St. Mary's, just as they had on Friday. It was a large funeral mass, with about fifty priests involved. Some of those at the front of the church were crying as Bishop Troy spoke for everyone. "We are shocked and filled with revulsion, but we must not be afraid, we must not give in."

Monsignor George Martin, president of St. Thomas University in Fredericton and a friend of Father Smith's for more than forty years, delivered the homily. "We have lost a friend, a good pastor, and a gentle man. The person or persons who have done this thing have violated their own humanity, their own dignity, the very humanity and very dignity that Father Smith affirmed all his life, by the proclamation of the gospel of Jesus Christ."

The procession was led by Vince Pineau, an assistant

to Father Smith for years. Pineau held the cross firmly erect as he marched slowly out of the church, the body of the priest following in the closed casket. Unable to hold back tears, Pineau pressed his face hard against the cross.

Father Smith's casket was taken to the cemetery where his father, mother, and sister are buried, the cemetery beside the church where he'd been baptized sixty-nine years before.

The snow began to fall ever more heavily as they placed the casket in the ground. Leonard took out a vial filled with the red earth of Cardigan, Prince Edward Island – Slim Jim's first parish, a place he returned to each summer – and sprinkled it on his brother's grave.

THIRTEEN

Guns under the Bed

AT THE VERY moment parishioners were discovering the murder of Father James Smith, members of the jury of the 1987 trial of Allan Legere were meeting with the RCMP in Newcastle.

The meeting started at 7 P.M. at the detachment office. Ron and his wife, Lois (not their real names), arrived punctually, full of questions about why they had been summoned.

They had no idea about Father Smith and would not until they went home. The police said nothing about the murder, which was reported to them just as the meeting was starting.

Ron had never been on a jury before the Legere trial. The three-week case thrust him into the limelight, and he was glad to get out of it when the trial ended. His life and that of his family had returned to normal. The only hitch occurred when he received a letter from Legere's lawyer asking for a meeting.

"He wanted to know if I'd known Allan Legere before the trial. I heard the name before the trial, but I really didn't know a thing about him." There was no meeting, and that was the end of it – until May 3, 1989, the day Legere escaped.

The fear built slowly. Ron had heard the rumours that Legere might come back and try to wreak revenge on those who had helped jail him for life. But the idea seemed rather far-fetched.

"I wasn't too concerned because I figured they'd catch him before too long. Then it was one week and two weeks. Then as time went on and especially after Father Smith, that's when you started getting real depressed, because you wondered if they're going to catch him. You got thinking, they might never catch that guy."

Ron had closely followed the news of the hunt for Legere through the streets and woods of Chatham. Like many others, he couldn't understand why it was taking so long to capture him.

Then, on May 29, Annie Flam was murdered, her sister-in-law Nina assaulted, and their downtown Chatham home set on fire. There was talk that Legere might be involved, but who could say for sure? Police acknowledged that they wanted to question Legere in the case, but they also wanted to talk to David and John Tanasichuk, two other escapees.

Though the fear didn't entirely go away, Ron, like most people in the area, concentrated on his work and enjoying the summer.

Summer slid into fall. A pair of attacks in Newcastle didn't upset Ron too much. Morrissy Doran was shot during an attempted robbery at his home on September 30. It was rumoured that his attacker had threatened to shove him in the deepfreeze unless Doran did what he was told. The next night, just down the street from Doran's home, Edwin and Evangeline Russell were attacked in their house. They apparently escaped only when the struggle in the home spilled out into the street and the man ran away, leaving a gun behind. The rumour mill, already in high gear, spread the word that the attacker had told the Russells that he wasn't there to rob them, but to hurt them.

Still, the police drew no link between the attacks and Legere, and that was enough to let Ron sleep peacefully each night. Until, that is, Donna and Linda Daughney were found sexually assaulted and beaten in their burning home, barely a minute's walk from the Russell home in downtown Newcastle.

The lack of information the police provided frustrated Ron. "I often wondered why they didn't have a PR man to tell people what they are allowed to tell them. I know they can't tell people everything because it's going to hurt their investigation, but it would have helped a little bit. In a case of that kind, people are looking for information.

"I didn't buy a scanner. I'd like to have had one, but then I would have got no sleep at all. I'd have stayed up all night listening to it."

It took police nearly two weeks after the Daughney episode to announce, on October 24, that Legere was a suspect in the murder and a prime suspect in the Flam attack.

Ron, had reached that conclusion the moment he'd heard about the Daughney killing. The images from the pictures shown to him during the 1987 trial flooded back into his mind. There was John Glendenning's body sprawled behind a bedroom door in his rural home. There was the blood.

There was also Ron's memory of Legere, the way the killer stared at the jury, seemingly for hours at a time without a break, except to write something on the paper in front of him. Ron did his best to ignore him, making a point of not looking at him, but every time he stole a glance Legere was there, staring. Ron began to give in to the fear.

Ron's son, Mark (not his real name), had bought a pup, intending to use the dog for the 1990 hunting season. To house-train the animal, someone had to take him out several times a day. Often, that someone was Lois.

"I didn't want to scare her," Ron remembered. "I didn't tell her how I felt for quite a while. But she would get up in the night with him at, say, two o'clock, put on her coat and go outside with him all alone. I didn't like to tell her not to do it, but finally I had to. I said, 'Don't you go out that door with that dog.' She knew then that I was pretty nervous."

She also took the hint. "When she found out I was concerned, I could see where she was being more careful. Every day I'd come home and the door would be locked. It was never locked in the daytime. But then when I came home in the day she'd be in the kitchen working and the door would be locked.

"Her and I sat down and talked about it a lot, but you can talk about it, but what can you do? You couldn't do much. You still had to carry on with your life.

"I told her that when she was here during the day, that when you're going to the car make sure you take a look around. Make sure all the doors are locked in the car. Don't leave a door unlocked."

They had kept a rifle under their bed for years, ever since a man accidentally walked into their home late one night thinking it was another house. Though the gun was never loaded, its bullets were kept within easy reach.

Now Lois told Ron: "You'd better load that gun."

"So I loaded it. Then Mark spoke to me. He has two or three guns, and he said, 'Do you want one of mine?' So I got one of his and brought it down.

"I kept two loaded guns underneath my bed. One was a shotgun with a slug in it and the other was a high-powered .22 using magnum bullets. It had seven shells in it."

The fear spread to his son.

"One night I was snoring in there and Mark could hear me," Ron recalled, pointing in the direction of the den. "I stopped snoring, and when I did Lois started coughing. That scared him so bad that he come out of bed and tiptoed down with the gun and peeked in to see if we were all right.

"Mark used to take the dog out at night, and he would shove a long knife up underneath his sleeve before going out. I seen him doing it."

When the RCMP called to ask Ron and his wife to come to the meeting at the detachment office on November 16, they were eager. They went, looking for answers. About half of the jury from the 1987 trial showed up. Some had moved away, some didn't bother to show up.

Some of those present were more nervous than others. "I talked to one of the jurymen that night, one of the guys that lived in Chatham, and he didn't sleep at all at night. He sat up with a loaded gun and let his wife sleep." He had reason to be nervous. It was his former home where a gunman had appeared on October 28 and broken into a car, apparently in search of indentification papers.

"We questioned them about why they had asked us in," Ron recalled. "They said, 'Well, we're going to do the same with a lot of groups of people.' What we were trying to pin down was if they knew something we didn't. It just seemed to us that they were calling the jury in to tell us more or less that we had to start protecting ourselves. What it all amounted to was telling us how to secure our houses."

Cpl. Lev Jackson from Fredericton did most of the talking at the detachment office. Sgt. Ernie Munden was supposed to be there too, but came in late and left quickly. He ended up spending much of the night in Chatham Head talking to reporters about the murder of Father Smith.

Jackson informed the jurors of ways to make their homes safer. It was pretty basic stuff – make sure basement windows are properly locked, put deadbolts on doors. Pamphlets on home security also were distributed.

"But he more or less told us that night," Ron recalled, "that if Allan Legere wanted to break into your house, there was nothing you could do to stop him. His words were, 'He's an expert escape artist.' He said he would probably sit on a hill somewhere and study someone's house for a month. He would sit across the street and watch your house for a month. He would know that house inside out without ever being inside of it." Despite all this, the RCMP avoided explicitly saying that the jurors were potential targets.

Ron's wife wasn't satisfied. "I asked quite a few questions, but she's really good at that. She asked a lot of questions. She wanted to know how come they asked the jurors back there. It just looked like maybe the jurors had been threatened.

"They said, 'Well, we called you people in, then we're going to call a crowd into the town hall." He didn't say who, but they were going to explain the same thing to them. He did tell us that night that the prosecutor was threatened." (Jackson was referring to Fred Ferguson, prosecutor in the Glendenning case, whom police were protecting.)

Ron never did finish reading the pamphlet on home security. His phone rang shortly after he got home from the meeting. The caller told him what had happened in Chatham Head to Father Smith. It seemed there was nowhere left to turn.

His daughters in Alberta and Nova Scotia were calling home more frequently, collect. The phone bill for part of October and November was close to $250. "They just kept calling to say 'How are you making out? Are you worried? Are you scared? What are you going to do?'"

He didn't know what he was going to do. He even considered leaving the area for a while, but dismissed the idea.

"It got so bad here. We were putting down this hardwood floor, and there were two or three days we had to get out, we couldn't stay here. And I stayed down with relatives at night. Mark went to the camp. Lois went to her mother's. And at four-thirty in the morning I'd get up and come up here to get ready because I went to work at six. I wanted to warm the place up. I had no car. I had to walk. It's only a quarter of a mile, but I'm going to tell you, from the time I left there to the time I got up here I didn't lose any time. I was pretty scared. Coming down to the last week, every little creak in the house at night, we were lying awake."

Ron talked about the anxiety with a brother from time to time, but that didn't help too much either. It was easy to tell the brother was also worried. Frank (not his real name) also kept a gun at home. And when the dog whined at some stranger walking down their street at night, he would jump out of bed. There was even a search in his area and one night a policeman came to his door to have a look around.

A call from the RCMP inadvertently made the stress worse, Ron said. "They told us that they had our house under surveillance, but they didn't tell the others that they had them under surveillance. Lois was talking to one of the jurors' wives and they never got no call."

Ron wondered if he was being singled out for a reason. "You run it through your mind what you'd do if something happened. You lay at night and think about it. I kept thinking about the way they broke into John Glendenning's house. They just smashed the door and in they come. So you start figuring out how you're going to work it if they come in. It mightn't be like that, but that's the way I had it planned if they come in.

"I was right over me gun and I was just going to flop down behind the bed and I was just going to lay it down on the bed. I was going to take Lois with me. I didn't tell her that. I was just going to grab her and haul her down behind the bed. I was going to use the bed as a shield.

"I'm not a gun man. I shot one deer in me life, that was back when I was eighteen or twenty, and I knew that wasn't for me and I never hunted after, maybe shot the odd partridge. But after this started happening I often thought what would I say if somebody asked me could I shoot a man.

"Up until this episode, I know I would have said no way could I shoot a man, there'd just be no way. But you know, during the last few weeks of that, I think I could have shot him if he'd come through the door. If he come through the door and I knew it was him."

FOURTEEN

Locked Doors and Hidden Hammers

EVERYTHING changed for Tom and Betty (not their real names) the morning of Saturday, October 14.

The weekend looked like it might be pleasant for the time of year, cool, but not rainy. Not the kind of weekend you'd want to be working. But Tom worked at the pulp and paper mill, and it was his turn for the weekend shift.

Like most people in their Newcastle neighbourhood, they'd followed the news closely after the murder of Annie Flam. It was a terrible crime, they knew, but it seemed a bit remote, despite having happened just six miles downriver. They didn't know Flam. There was talk about Allan Legere being a suspect, but it didn't fit. Why would he stick around the one place where police were trying so hard to catch him? It didn't make sense.

They'd heard, too, about the numerous sightings of Legere in the area in the past six months and had read about the attacks two weeks before of Morrissy Doran and Edwin and Evangeline Russell. Certainly the kind of thing to make older people nervous, but Tom and Betty aren't seniors, so it didn't hit home too hard.

Tom's work often took him out of town and Betty

stayed home alone in their bungalow. Neither one thought much about it. They'd been doing that for years. There were never any problems.

They lived in one of the older neighbourhoods in town, had been there close to twenty years. They had raised their children in that house, watched their son play road hockey on the street. Neighbours looked out for neighbours. True, there was trouble several years ago when thieves broke into a few cars and homes. They locked the doors to the house after that but, with neighbours on all sides, that was about all the precaution they took.

The sons of a nextdoor neighbour used to park a truck in Tom's yard when he was away so anyone going by would think he was still home. Another neighbour, this one living at the other end of their short street, told Betty one night that he always made a point of watching out for her when he knew Tom was away on business. It was easy to feel safe.

At the same time, Betty's brother, Sam, nagged her to be more careful, to lock the doors during the day. "I used to laugh at him," she recalled. "I'd say better to leave your door open so people will think you're at home."

Their sense of safety vanished after the murders of the Daughney sisters. Tom was in the mill when he heard about the killings. He hoped it was just more of the usual gossip, something the mill was well known for. Some people just loved to make up a story and watch it zip among the hundreds of workers on each shift. That irritated Tom. It could be vicious, a cruel way to have fun. In his twenty-odd years there, he had always gone out of his way to ignore the rumours and never to help spread them.

This story proved different. Some people made a few calls. It turned out to be true.

Tom called Betty. "I'm not going away anywhere from now on," he told her.

His reaction surprised his wife. "I've never seen him so cautious, because things like that don't usually bother him a lot."

When Tom came home he looked at the house differently, trying to think like an attacker, searching for weak points. The windows were obvious ones, especially the basement windows. Of particular concern was a window under the sundeck at the back of the house. He blocked that off by nailing shut the small door in the lattice-work beneath the sundeck platform.

The upstairs windows were next. They had been put in years before, when sliding windows were popular. They had clasp locks, of course, but how often had they heard stories about how easy those locks were to jimmy? Tom put a block of wood in each window in the house, jamming each one shut.

"We also blocked off our sliding door with chairs," Betty said. "We thought if they did get in, at least we'd hear the racket. We put kitchen chairs right up against the doors. We talked about getting an alarm, but we didn't get one because I said to Tom if he ever was away and I heard that alarm, it would scare me to death."

Betty also refused to buy a gun. Yet for all her efforts at burglar-proofing, she remained worried about what to do if someone broke in. She cornered Sgt. Ernie Munden following the public meeting in Newcastle a few days after the Daughney killings. "I said, 'It would be pretty scary if I were in the house alone and somebody walked into the bedroom. If it was Allan Legere, or anybody else, what would you do if you didn't have a gun?'

"He said, 'Ask him what he wants.'"

That answer didn't make her feel any better, but she did agree that a gun might aggravate an attacker, make the situation worse. Moreover, "I just couldn't bear the thoughts of killing anybody, deliberately shooting someone. I don't think I could do it. Unless," she said, looking at her husband, "someone was trying to kill you. Then I might be able to do it."

Guns and alarms out of the question, they improvised another means of defence. Betty kept a hammer at her side of the bed. Tom found an eleven-pound pipe wrench, which he placed on the floor at his bedside.

They changed their daily routine too. Betty, a teacher, started to come home a few minutes later each day after school, never getting there before Tom, who hurried home first. "And when I came home," Tom recalled, "the first thing I did was go downstairs and check everything out, the closets, everything."

The fear began to play with their minds. One night Betty went to the back door, which opens directly into an alcove and stairs to a renovated basement. "Tom said, 'You didn't lock that back door?' I was certain I had, but sometimes, if you don't pull it real tight, it doesn't lock. We went down and looked in every room. We thought somebody could have come in. I was so sure I had locked the door that we thought somebody had done something and was hiding in the basement. We even looked in the coal cellar."

Another time their neighbour told them about a damaged screen over a basement window. Someone had cut it along the edges, as if preparing to break in, yet Betty and Tom had heard nothing. "The neighbours have a dog, and if anything goes on at night, that thing goes wild," Tom said.

"He's a big German shepherd," added his wife, "and I'm glad they have him. At least it's a warning."

Sleeping proved difficult for Betty. Her imagination refused to take a break. She kept drawing mental images of what must have happened to the Daughney sisters on their last night. "We always shut our lights off at night before, every night. But after the Daughneys, we left on every light we could have on, even the light over the stove," Tom said. "And everybody along the street did the same. It was just like daytime here."

The killing of Father Smith changed Tom's sleeping habits. "I'd hear creaks and wake up in the middle of the night. I was a sound sleeper. The house would fall down and I'd never hear it, but not anymore."

Like many Miramichi residents, the couple found it impossible to relax. Danger, real and imagined, was always on their minds. They disliked leaving the house, fearing what might be awaiting them when they returned. "When we went out at night, we'd leave all the lights on and leave the radio on," Tom said. "I remember us noticing that the town looked so strange because there was nobody walking around hardly. One Friday evening we went downtown about ten and we saw one person."

The fear affected their work and the people with whom they worked. Tom noticed it among colleagues at the mill when something broke and had to be fixed immediately, regardless of the hour. "If I got a call from the mill in the middle of the night to go up, I wouldn't go. A lot of people refused to go if there was a breakdown. They'd say, 'Look, I'm sorry, but with my wife and kids, I just can't do it.' When my boss asked me, 'If you got a call, would you come in?' I said, 'No, I wouldn't.'"

At a meeting of millworkers, there was talk of forcing people to report for work. Eventually, supervisors worked out an informal system whereby they called in individuals who had someone else in the home, or nearby friends they could call to stay with their family.

In the meantime, Tom started to cancel business trips that had been set up long before, trips to Moncton, Halifax, and Newfoundland. "I had to go to Fredericton, and I called up and said, 'I'm sorry, but I don't think I'll be able to go. If anything ever happened I just couldn't live with myself.' There was no point in me going because I wouldn't have been able to concentrate on what I was doing anyway."

Betty tried to talk him out of the cancellations, but failed. "I don't like the idea of leaving the house when he's away, but I wouldn't have liked the idea of staying alone either. I doubt if I would have slept very much."

They noticed the strain the fear was having on friends and acquaintances. "We have a little new teacher in her twenties at our school, a music teacher from Sussex. She was terrified," Betty recalled. "Her parents wanted her to resign, they were so worried about her. She lived in an apartment by herself. One of the other teachers had to go and stay with her after the Daughney murders. The teacher stayed there the whole time. The little one couldn't stay alone. She told us. Her parents pleaded with her to resign so she could get away from it."

At her elementary school, Betty would "give the kids a chance to talk about it if they wanted to. One little fellow in Grade 4 was real concerned. The reward money was being raised. 'Some people won't tell,' the little lad said. 'The reason they won't tell is they're waiting for the reward money to go up higher.' He'd tell me about noises his mother heard at home and calling the police. I even heard the kids in Grade 1 in the hall talking about Allan Legere."

Added Tom, "There was a woman over in Loggieville, near Chatham, who was ninety-three. She lived by herself. They had an awful time with her. She refused to leave her home until after the Smith murder. As soon as they caught Legere, she went right back the next day."

"It must have been harder for seniors to understand," Betty said, finishing his thought. "They lived in a time when it was even more gentle than when we were growing up."

Another senior who moved was Allan Legere's mother. When her son escaped custody in May, Louise Legere phoned the Moncton police department to say that they should not have described him as armed and dangerous. While she accepted her son's "involvement" in the Glendenning affair, she was reluctant to believe he would do "something as horrible as murder."

However, as the terror gripped the Miramichi in the fall and police named her son as a prime suspect, the feisty seventy-year-old, fearing for her life, decided to move to Ottawa. She stayed with one of her two daughters. The daughter's husband, ironically, was a civilian employee of the RCMP.

In the meantime, advice from relatives poured into Tom and Betty. "The kids were always warning me to not dare to stay alone, for one thing. My sister in the southern U.S. and my brother in Nova Scotia warned me not to dare stay alone. They couldn't believe it either. Newcastle and Chatham were always nice quiet places to them growing up."

One thing Tom and Betty did not consider was moving away. "It would have had to be an awful lot worse and, even then, I don't think I could," Betty said. The Miramichi was home, had been home for Betty and her family for generations. She was prepared to stay and tough it out. She was brought up to respect her elders and the authorities, particularly the police. She read the criticisms of their handling of the case, heard comments on the television and in the streets, and felt sorry for the officers she was certain were doing their best.

"But every time I heard that thing about somebody harbouring Allan Legere, that used to make me mad. That was like saying it was our fault that the police aren't getting anywhere."

FIFTEEN

"I Want a .357"

GORD CHRISTIE remembered all the lights after Father Smith was killed.

Christie works the morning shift at CFAN, the private radio station in Newcastle. He has been there for close to ten years. His day starts early, around five o'clock. Christie followed his usual work pattern right through the months of fear. He'd leave his apartment on the third floor of a large home on what used to be Newcastle's main street, walk down the street, then stop in at the local Irving gas station.

On the morning of Friday, November 17, he looked out over the town spread below his apartment. "It was like Christmas," he recalled. Lights were on everywhere, lights he'd never noticed before, lights that had been left on the entire night. The sight was to become a familiar one over the next ten days.

Christie – well known in the area for his radio work and for emcee appearances at variety shows and beauty contests – knew how frightened people were. He had watched it build since October, when the Daughney sisters were found murdered in their home, just a five-minute walk from his apartment.

People familiar with Christie's early-morning routine started looking for him, stopping him on their way to or from work, eager to hear if he knew anything they hadn't yet heard. Christie's voice was so familiar that some would suddenly blurt out their fears. One man admitted to him: "I find myself locking my doors when I'm driving down the streets."

Another time Christie met a man out for a walk, keeping up a routine established long before the killing started. "You're not letting all of this bother you, I see," Christie said.

"Oh, yes. We have everything timed," came the reply. "If I'm not back by 7:35, they'll come looking for me."

Christie's work often calls for him to do live broadcasts from local businesses, the demand for which usually increases as Christmas nears. But as 1989 drew to a close, the fear was hurting business on the Miramichi. One grocery store operator told Christie, "I might as well send the cashiers home at night, there's nobody around here."

A pair of late November concerts featuring Irish tenor Frank Patterson ran into trouble when ticket sales sagged. Patterson was well known in the area, having sung to packed audiences at the Irish festival held each summer. Now people were afraid to leave their homes once the sun went down. Organizers had to make an extra effort to fill the seats, even though one of the concerts was a benefit to raise money for the reward established to fight the wave of killings.

The fear even touched Patterson personally. A man fitting the general description of Allan Legere showed up in the hall outside the restaurant in the motel where the singer and his family were staying. The man scanned the room, as if looking for someone, then left, only to return a minute later to look again. Patterson, who was eating, was so unnerved that he quickly looked around for something with which he might defend his family. The man disappeared again. The singer left a day later for his New York home. There, he beefed up security. He also made a point of calling a friend in Newcastle frequently over the ensuing days to see how the search for Legere was going.

People's personalities began to change, Christie felt. They were depressed, frustrated by an urgent need to do *something* when there was nothing they could do. It was as if they were collectively saying, "How long are we going to suffer?"

A member of the local gun club, the Miramichi Sportsmens' Club, Christie was particularly worried about the sudden interest in guns among people who clearly knew little about them. A middle-aged woman came up to him seeking advice. She was upset because her son had bought a gun. She didn't like the idea of having weapons in her home. She wanted to know what she might do to convince him to get rid of it.

Christie could do little more than suggest that she remind him of the dangers of owning a weapon and the legal implications if he shot someone. He couldn't tell if the advice helped; the woman looked relieved at simply being able to talk about it with someone.

Later an elderly man came up to him. He was obviously upset. "I had to make a disturbing decision yesterday," he told Christie. "I hate guns, but I bought one anyway. Now I'm not sure if I'm more frightened of the gun or Legere, but I'm too old to fend off anyone coming into my home."

Christie came to call these people "hostages to the gun." Owners of gun shops felt hamstrung when people came through the door with the proper papers needed to buy a gun, but with no knowledge of what they were getting.

One day, a man in his mid-sixties walked up to the counter of one such store and said, "I want a .357."

"What kind, sir?" the clerk asked. "A Colt?"

"I don't know. Just a .357. That's what I was told I should buy."

The incident upset the store owner. "Jesus, I hate selling guns to someone like that," he told Christie later.

Christie had weapons in his own home, of course, but they weren't loaded. "That's not to say I didn't think about it a lot. They were within easy reach, so was the ammunition."

The edginess seemed pervasive. Two retired teachers, both in their eighties were living near Christie when one evening one of them had a nightmare. Her scream awakened the other woman, who grabbed a poker and ran into the room. Later she said she was amazed at how calm she had felt. "I knew I was going to get one good swing in," she said.

The fear also seemed to affect people's good judgement. When a rumour spread that a doughnut-shop operator had been implicated in a series of attacks on seniors, one woman asked Christie for the latest news about his arrest. When told that there would be no arrest because the story was untrue, the woman became indignant. "I was there. I saw the whole thing," she said.

You couldn't be too angry with such individuals, said Christie. They were so desperate for the terror to end that they were ready to accept anyone as the killer.

SIXTEEN

"What He Done to My Son"

"HE NEVER GOT a break in his life, my young lad, because he's got to follow my name. My name is Matchett, they're going to take him as a Matchett. It's a reputation."

Billy Matchett sat at his round kitchen table talking about his life, the life of his son, and the man he's known for more than twenty years – Allan Legere.

Billy is fifty-one, under five foot six, with a belly that shows the signs of too many afternoons raising too many glasses of beer. He combs his grey hair forward, covering his forehead, making him seem even shorter than he is. His face is very round, almost a circle. His moustache is the same colour as his hair.

Barefoot, dressed in grey sweatpants and a gray sweatshirt that didn't quite cover his belly, he apologized for the condition of his home on McArthur Street in the south end of Newcastle. From the outside it looked like any other bungalow on the street, except there were no Christmas decorations, only three large chunks of raw meat on the front step. They were for the pit bull terrier he had bought after Legere escaped – and after two of his dogs mysteriously disappeared.

The interior of the house was a mess, the result of a fire in October. Firefighters had put out the flames before too much damage was done. There was furniture everywhere, even a red office divider.

Billy thought he knew who set fire to his house the one night he wasn't home. His priorities in repairing it were set accordingly. The front door, for example, was red and made of steel. For a time, Billy strung a thick piece of chain through an eye hook on one side of the door, back and down through another eye hook, then across to another door. If anyone tried to break in by kicking down the front door, the chain would hold the door in place long enough for Billy to get his gun.

There was another difference between Billy's house and the others on the street. Except for the living-room window and the sliding patio doors by the kitchen, there were iron bars on all the windows – in the kitchen, bathroom, bedrooms, and downstairs. They were new too, added since the fire. If Legere came after him, there would be only two ways in, Billy figured.

Billy has a reputation, a bad one, and he admits it freely. "It just grew on me, I guess." A reputation as a fence? "Yeah, I had that. Been never proven. I was called down at the court as being the biggest gangster in New Brunswick and the biggest hot goods distributor in Canada."

But, Billy says, he retired "from all that stuff years ago." There's no money in it now. Besides, he wanted to be a good example to his son, Todd. "I was trying to show my young lad that there's no money in the other side. You got to get into the legal side to be into the money. Because dishonest money is no good to you. It's money to spend real fast."

Todd Matchett is doing life without hope of parole for at least sixteen years. A jury says he helped kill John Glendenning. Billy doesn't see it that way. He blames Legere.

When Legere got out of prison on mandatory supervision in 1985, he came to Billy to buy a car from him. He kept coming back. The two men knew each other well. Perhaps too well.

"I kept telling him that since he's coming here, with my name, that they'd be watching me, they'd be watching him. I didn't want no bad business."

According to Matchett, Legere was more interested in his son, and in Todd's friend Scott Curtis. He tried to warn his son about his newfound friend, telling him, "'If Allan ever comes up with any ideas, stay clear of him. Don't do anything with him. Don't do nothing with him.' I tried to warn my young lad and Scott. I tried to warn both of them."

Sure, Billy said, Todd had a record, but it was always for minor offences. But Legere took him "from the little time to the big time," and that's unforgiveable.

Matchett's voice sounded resigned as he described what happened. "I knew Allan, but I should have known him a little bit better. I should've known he was too smart for them. He went behind my back. This man is dangerous. My young lad, I hammered it into him fifty times. Legere sucked him in a little at a time. He's smart that way. He's a professional at that game."

Todd Matchett didn't help plan the Glendenning affair or get any money out of it, Billy maintains. Legere, by contrast, has always said Billy did.

After the robbery, Todd and Scott fled to Toronto. Billy said he heard about the robbery and murder on the radio, added it all up, and convinced the boys to turn themselves in. "The young lads didn't have the initiative to go down and pull something like that. If they had robbed the Royal Bank, I'd be clapping them on the back. They woulda went to jail. I'd of respected them. To go to jail for this kind of crime, I would never go for something like that."

What Legere told Todd and Scott was, 'Come on, we're going to run in, we're going to grab a money box, and we're going to run out. That's it.' Well, that wasn't it. Legere went in there, he didn't go in there for no money box. He went in there because he wanted to hurt somebody."

When the trial came, the boys pleaded guilty. Legere, in his testimony, said Todd and Scott had done everything, that he was the bystander. Legere violated that code among criminals that says "Never snitch." Said Matchett: "Legere's a rat. He proved that in court by testifying against them lads. They pleaded guilty. It don't mean he had to testify against them."

Allan Legere and Billy Matchett are enemies, according to Billy. From the time of Legere's escape in May 1989, Billy barely slept. He waited for Legere to come for him. "Allan, he's about the person I'd be most scared of in my lifetime. With loaded guns. I figured he'd come here. Account of Todd, account of Scott, he would love to take me down a notch. By killing me."

Billy is convinced that at least one attempt was made on his life, after the October fire. The attempt failed only because he had the dog, traps around the house, bars on the windows, and left the patio door and front window "weak."

It started with a crack. Billy was in the basement, but he heard it. "I came up the stairs, seen someone at the window. Went back down. I got my rifle. Back up again. The rifle was already loaded. I couldn't get the bolt ahead. The bolt locked on me. So I just took the gun, pointed it at him and he jumped over and ran."

"For what Legere done to my son, I would've killed him. I would've taken the consequences. My son realizes that he's in prison because he didn't listen to me, 'cause he tells me."

SEVENTEEN

The Love of the Chase

WITH THE murder of Father James Smith, fear turned to panic.

Just hours after the body of Father Smith was found, reporters jammed into a room at the Newcastle town hall to hear what police had to say. Sergeant Munden refused to comment when asked whether or not a weapon was used.

Asked why it seemed that Legere was still hanging around the Miramichi in spite of the increased police presence, Munden speculated: "This individual, he loves the chase. He thrives on the attention. He loves the chase."

However, finding Father Smith's car in Bathurst near the train station after the murder had planted a seed of doubt about where to look. "Up until last night, I believed he was in the area. Today, I'm not certain," Munden confessed.

Police released a sketch of a man suspected of helping Legere. The drawing was of a thin man, possibly twenty to twenty-five years old, with a long face and nose. His cheeks were pitted with what appeared to be acne scars or moles. His hair was described as being reddish-brown and straight. His eyes were distinctively light, perhaps blue or green. He was tall, about six feet, but with narrow shoulders. Still, he was described as having a large bone structure. He had a patchy beard and moustache.

The sketch was big news. Police had speculated all along that Legere was getting help from someone, but could offer no evidence why they thought so, other than to say that there had to be an accomplice for Legere to avoid capture for so long. That suggestion angered many, who felt the community was being unfairly blamed for harbouring a convicted killer. The sketch, however, was so specific. It seemed as if someone must have had a good look at the man, perhaps even known him. This was no typical sketch that might look like any of hundreds of local people. It was too precise for that.

In fact, to former Chatham police chief Dan Allen, it looked very much like someone he knew. Allen was well known for his ability to get inside the head of a criminal, to see the world through the eyes of the man he was after. Now he started to mentally turn the illustration around until he could picture the face in profile. He added weight to that profile. Yes, Allen thought, the drawing could be only one man: Allan Legere.

True, it was a Legere thirty or forty pounds lighter than the one he knew, but that was a distinct possibility if he was living in the woods and stealing whatever food he could find.

Allen told the RCMP his conclusions. The idea was a shocker, but Allen's credibility was high. Police agreed that their focus would remain Legere. Any search for an accomplice would take a back seat.

The hunt intensified with startling speed. Police refused to say if it was true that officers were camping in woods, hiding in sleeping bags, waiting. They also refused to say if a special search team had been flown in from British Columbia.

This refusal to comment was pointless. People could see for themselves. There were police officers and cars everywhere. Outside Chatham, the building housing the major crime unit was surrounded by cars and four-wheel-drive trucks every day. At night, they disappeared, dispatched to patrol various key points.

Concerns about dollars and budgets vanished. Whatever you need, you get, period, the politicians said. The enormous display of men and machinery drove the point home.

What was most noticeable was the RCMP's Emergency Response Team, the ERT squad. A highly specialized, highly trained unit of ten men, they spent all of October and November searching for the killer, sometimes for twenty-four hours at a stretch. Easily visible in their dark uniforms during the day, they became invisible at night. They often slept in the woods, enduring freezing temperatures, unable to set fires for warmth in case they were spotted, hoping for that one chance. They were armed with heavy-calibre weapons, knives, and special night vision equipment.

Still, demands for military assistance persisted. Circle the area, use as many men as you need, comb it inch by inch. Get him. Whatever it takes, get him.

The RCMP's response was always the same. What do you surround and search, when you don't know where to look? Their lack of success frustrated RCMP officers flown in from across the country, away from their families for weeks at a stretch. One eight-year-old boy sent his officer father a note that said, "I love you, even if you're never home."

Searches were launched at the slightest provocation. On November 18, little more than a day after Father Smith was found, police circled an area west of Chatham. Reporters scrambled to find out what was going on. It turned out to be a reporter from a daily paper and a friend out for a walk in the woods. Angry police later suggested privately that the stunt was an attempt to test the response time of the police.

November 19 brought cold weather and snow. With it came hope. No longer could woodsmens' tricks work against men and dogs. A dog's nose might be fooled by doubling back, but no man could walk on snow and not leave a trail of footprints. Plus, it was cold. Few persons could hide for long in a tent or lean-to in the foul weather that grabbed the region like a vicious fist.

A worker in a half-ton truck spotted a bearded man matching photos of Legere sneaking around a cross-country ski club's clubhouse several miles north of Newcastle. The driver headed down the hill, hoping to get a better look, and nearly ran the man down as he bolted in front of the truck. The man leaped over the snow bank and vanished into the woods. Confusion about where the sighting was delayed a search by about two hours, but police, dogs, and a helicopter soon blanketed the area.

The man had been wearing a checkered shirt, had carried a gun, and had a large knife strapped to a leg. "He looked right at me when he ran past," the eyewitness said. "He had this look on his face, he looked terrified."

People hugged their scanners, praying that this

would be the finale, keenly aware that it was early afternoon and the light would fade in a couple of hours. Some people living in subdivisions a half mile north of the sighting moved out as the chopper headed their way.

Around dark word shot from house to house, phone to phone: they had him! He was in a police car behind a mall! Unfortunately, the "he" turned out to be a hunter out looking for rabbit.

Rumours continued to feed rumours. *Miramichi Leader* editor Rick MacLean was moving that week. His house had been sold months earlier, with the deal set to close that Friday, November 24, and the movers coming Monday night. One day he received a call from a Chatham resident. "Was it true?" he was asked.

"Was what true?"

"That you're moving out, that the police say you'd better leave because you've been saying all those things about Legere on the television."

With much of the community unwilling to appear in front of a camera for fear of being singled out, reporters looking for someone to interview turned to MacLean. He appeared on radio and TV programs ranging from CBC's "Morningside" to CTV's "Canada AM." MacLean told one reporter he was taking precautions, but he wasn't ready to be bullied into changing his lifestyle. Despite the brave talk, the changes came – getting home before dark, checking doors two or three times.

As pressure mounted, the *Toronto Sun* ran a story about fighting between police forces that was hindering the investigation. "Police Feud in N.B. Killer Hunt," blared the Page One headline of November 20. "Police in-fighting is the reason a fugitive killer hasn't been caught, municipal sources here say," read the story by Tom Godfrey. "Officers who don't want to be identified told the *Sun* there are deep rifts between them and the RCMP in the manhunt for convicted killer Allan Legere. The officers said the rift exists over the lack of information-sharing by the Mounties.

"Local police complain the Mounties have taken over the investigation and they've been phased out. 'We have the informants and sources in place, but we can't do anything with the information they give us. It's a one-way street because the Mounties aren't sharing anything with us,'" Godfrey quoted a police officer as saying.

It was a potent criticism, as Miramichi residents had already been wondering about the effectiveness of RCMP officers from places as far away as Ottawa who didn't know anything about the area. Sergeant Munden denied any rift and described the relationship between departments as good.

Meanwhile, police continued to assert that someone was hiding Legere. Why, the public asked, when it made no sense? It was too dangerous. Reasoned Munden, "He seems to possess the ability to motivate people to do things for him. There are people out there who don't believe he's guilty of anything."

The more dangerous it is, the more he likes it, Munden suggested. "This is a game of 'I can scare you, I can do what I want, and you can't catch me. I will outfox you.'"

It all seemed so futile. How could a man be out in that weather, his footprints clearly visible in the snow, and avoid capture? A police officer wearing combat fatigues and carrying an assault rifle with the word *Snake* on the stock compared it to a lottery. "It's like playing 6-49. One of these days, we're going to hit the jackpot." There was no choice but to keep playing.

Serial killers follow a pattern of striking again and again, says Elliott Leyton, a professor of sociology at Memorial University in Newfoundland and author of *Hunting Humans: The Rise of the Modern Multiple Murder*. It's not a question of if, but when.

"The normal pattern is they keep killing. Minor changes in victims are common. Whether the victims are male or female is insignificant. The time factor also means nothing. Serial killers choose a time that's convenient for them and changes in that pattern are common. They change patterns to get ahead of police."

His theory as to why some men become serial killers is starkly straightforward. Modern society strips away the high sense of value once placed on life, he writes. "The freedom for which mankind had struggled over the centuries proved to be a two-edged sword. The freedom from the suffocation of family and community, the freedom from systems of religious thought, the freedom to explore one's self, all entailed heavy penalities to society – not the least of which was the rate of multiple murder. Whether the industrial system was socialist or capitalist, its members were forced to look upon themselves and others as marketable commodities. It can hardly be surprising then that some fevered souls, feeling automatons, might choose to coalesce their fuzzy identity in a series of fearful acts. Their ambitions crushed, some would lash out in protest at objects (most often sexual) which they had been taught to see as essentially insignificant."

Add to this frightening picture the kind of upbringing shared by many serial killers. A disturbing majority of those Leyton looked at had a rootless childhood. They were either adopted, illegitimate, institutionalized in a mental or juvenile home, or had a mother married several times. Their sense of self-worth vanished along the way.

"At a certain point in his life," Leyton notes, "the future killer experiences a kind of internal *social* crisis, when he realizes that he cannot be what he wishes to be – cannot live his version of the American Dream." Frustrated by what he sees as a society that persecutes him at every turn, denies him the life that is justly his, he strikes back.

Sex is not the motivator, just an added benefit. Money is not the key either. Social status is the objective. Serial killers want a central place in their society, whatever size that society might be. They want to be famous, to be big shots. If killing is what it takes, so what. They don't see their victims as innocent, but as members of the group blocking the way to their just position in the community. The solution is to use murder to remake their society in such a way as to focus its attention on them.

Whether or not this analysis was correct, police and residents believed one thing: this killer, whoever he was, would strike again. The searches continued, day after day, night after night. And there was just one name on everyone's lips – Allan Legere.

Their efforts were in vain. Allan Legere was now hundreds of miles away from the Miramichi, relaxing in a room at the Queen Elizabeth Hotel in Montreal, a hotel that New Brunswick Premier Frank McKenna would later describe, only partly in jest, as too expensive for him to stay in when he travelled.

EIGHTEEN

Capture

JANE MEREDITH walked down Saint John's Prince William Street to her job as a barmaid at the Piper's Pub. It was just a few minutes before 11 A.M., Thursday, November 23, and already her first customer was waiting for her to unlock the door.

"Just your everyday person after a beer," she later recalled in the thick accent of her native Scotland.

The man was wearing a parka, woodsman's pants, and big heavy boots. He was cleanshaven, had medium-length black hair with grey streaks. He was also carrying a plastic shopping bag.

The man ordered a beer and sat in a corner table by the door next to a video machine. He was a good tipper and friendly. At noon, a policeman walked into the pub. The stranger didn't seem to notice.

Barmaid Judy Cook was playing a video game. The man wished her good luck. Someone asked where he came from. "Ottawa," replied the man. "What have you got in your bag?" someone else asked. "A gun," he said. Everyone laughed. He did, too.

The man kept drinking, a beer every sixty minutes. At supper time, rush-hour in Saint John, a car died on the street in front of the pub. The stranger went out, stopped traffic, and gave the driver a hand with the dead battery. He seemed to know cars. He got the vehicle working again, then returned to the pub.

He'd lost his glasses, but someone found them in the pub's washroom and gave them to the barmaid. She remembered the friendly man wearing them. He was thankful. "You don't have any idea how many I've broken or lost," he smiled.

He had a few more glasses of beer, played some more pool, then left around quarter to ten. He forgot – or left – something behind: a handwritten letter, fifteen pages long, lay on the table where he'd sat for most of the day. He'd signed his name, even put down his social insurance number. The style of handwriting was distinctive, small and cramped, angling slightly to the right. It was later handed over to police.

It was snowing heavily. Good weather for picking up fares, thought taxi driver Ron Gomke. He was twenty-one, and he'd been a cabbie for three weeks. It was better than working as a uniformed security guard for Burns Security in the shopping mall, his previous job. You didn't need a uniform to drive cab; just be yourself. Gomke was just under six feet tall, and weighed more than two hundred pounds. "A little hefty," he said later when asked to describe himself.

A man on the street hollered at Gomke. He stopped and looked back. A man walked towards the taxi, and got in beside him. The passenger wanted to go to Moncton.

Gomke called the dispatcher at ABC Taxi. "Car 20. Party going to Moncton. What's the fare?"

"One hundred dollars," said the dispatcher. "And get it up front."

Gomke was excited. A hundred dollars. Pretty good night's work.

The man fumbled through his pockets. Gomke looked out the window at the snow.

"We're going to Moncton," the man said.

Gomke turned. There was a rifle in the man's lap.

"This is a sawed-off .308. Tell them you've received the fare and do it in the calmest manner you can."

Gomke did as he was told. The rifle was in his ribs. They drove off.

"I'm the one they're looking for. I'm Allan Legere."

It's not clear how Legere had returned to New Brunswick from Quebec; perhaps he'd taken a train from Montreal to Saint John. However Legere had made it back made no difference to Gomke. He looked into the remarkably calm eyes staring at him and knew he was caught in a nightmare.

"If your dispatcher sends anyone, the moment the cruiser pulls us over, it's over for you," Legere told him, his voice so calm it was eerie. "I'll let you go if everything goes smooth. I want to go to Chatham, stay in a motel until six o'clock, then I want to go to the airport and hijack a plane to Iran."

Gomke agreed with everything. Legere kept talking, the gun always in his lap, always pointing at him. Gomke's father had died a few years before, and now his son was praying silently to him. I'm going to meet you soon, Dad. I'm going to meet you soon.

"Those cops," Legere snorted. "You have to laugh. They thought they were so close. They're so easy to elude. I lived in the woods, made friends with the chipmunks and squirrels. Hell, they ate right out of my hand."

Whatever you say, Gomke thought. Whatever you say.

"It was getting colder. I couldn't stay in the woods, I had to keep moving," Legere said. He talked about the murdered women, said he didn't kill them or the priest. Sure, he'd met the priest. He went to his house in the early eighties and told him it's not right to gamble. "The priest didn't like that. Chased me out of his house."

Drive the speed limit, Legere ordered. Gomke wanted to go slower because of the storm. Just outside Moncton, near Magnetic Hill, Gomke lost control of the taxi and went into a ditch.

"You've done it now," snarled Legere, "you've done it now. You've ruined my plans."

Michelle Mercer was driving home to Prince Edward Island. She was tired from the long drive from Montreal, from keeping her little Japanese car on the road because of the storm. She was a Mountie, on vacation, in civilian clothes.

Just ahead, her lights caught a man waving her down. She saw the taxi off the road in a bank of snow. She pulled over and got out.

"I'm a police officer. Can I help?" They needed a drive. She told the two men to get in her car. The skinnier one got in front, the bigger one in back.

Mercer wanted to pull off the road to rest. She suggested they stop at the nearest motel.

Her front-seat passenger said he'd lost his false teeth. They had to go back to the taxi. Mercer turned her car around. But then the man found his teeth in a pocket, so the car turned again, heading towards Moncton.

"I'm afraid you're going to have to do what I tell you," said the man in the seat beside her.

"What?" exclaimed Mercer.

"I'm the one they're looking for. I'm Allan Legere." The rifle was in his lap, pointing at her.

Legere told her to take the exit to Chatham. But she didn't know the roads, and the snow was coming down hard. She took an exit, but missed the turn to Chatham and ended up going back towards Saint John.

"You've got me all mixed up. You're trying to trick me," said Legere.

He calmed down, though. At one point he reached over and tousled Mercer's hair. She didn't like that and jerked her head away. Gomke sat in the back seat, not saying anything, afraid.

Mercer's car was getting low on fuel. They weren't going to get far if they didn't gas up. At Sussex, an hour south of Moncton in good weather, they pulled into the Four Corners Irving gas station alongside the Trans-Canada Highway. It was close to two in the morning.

Pump the gas, Legere told Mercer, then changed his mind. He took $20 from her, grabbed her keys, and locked the doors. Legere put in $15 worth of gas and went to pay.

Joy Levesque, twenty-four, was alone in the gas bar. "You must have the magic touch. That self-serve pump hasn't worked all week," she told Legere. He didn't reply.

In the car, Mercer turned to Gomke. "I've got a spare set of keys. Do you want to go for it?"

"Will he let us go?" asked Gomke. Mercer said she didn't think so, and there was no other chance.

"Then go for it. We've got nothing to lose," Gomke declared.

Mercer started the car and sped away. Legere was just

coming out of the gas bar, and he started to run after the car. Levesque thought they must be a married couple having an argument.

"Slow down, slow down," Gomke shouted at Mercer.

"Are you with him?" she shot back.

No, he said. She was just driving too fast for the road conditions, they'd end up in a ditch, and Legere would catch them.

She wanted to know where a police detachment was. He told her. The office was closed, but there was a phone box outside the front door for emergencies. Mercer went to the phone, gave her badge number and described what had happened.

Within minutes, police cruisers were at the gas station. A policeman jumped out and ran inside. He asked Levesque if she was all right. Sure, she said, but she didn't know why he was asking. He told her. She felt scared then.

Police searched the garage. One officer's rifle went off accidentally and blew a hole in the floor.

The word was out all over the province. Roadblocks were set up. He wasn't getting away this time. But where was he?

Legere was on the road to Moncton in a flatbed tractor-trailer. When Mercer and Gomke had escaped, Legere had run around the side of the gas station. There, Brian Golding was washing the windshield of his orange Mack truck.

"I'm Allan Legere, let's get going." He had a rifle.

They climbed in and drove off. Legere wouldn't let Golding stop at a truck weigh station on the way, even though the law required it. Golding switched on his flashers, hoping the weigh station attendant would notice and call police. No luck.

They turned north and headed to Chatham. As they neared the Miramichi, Legere told Golding to stop. They were going to wait until six o'clock, then go to the airport and take a plane, he explained. Golding told him that there were only propeller-driven planes there, so he wouldn't get far. They continued on their way. Later, Legere ordered Golding to pull off the highway onto a secondary road and disconnect the flatbed. They were just three miles from Newcastle.

Another truck driver saw the orange Mack truck on the road. He knew tractor-trailers didn't use that road, and he called police on his CB radio.

Get moving, Legere told Golding. They were on the Barnaby River Road. A police four-wheel-drive pulled in behind them, its lights flashing.

Keep driving, Legere ordered. Instead, Golding hit a button that locked the brakes, stopping the truck. He jumped out.

"Don't shoot, don't shoot, I'm not Allan Legere." With his curly hair and moustache, Golding could have passed for Legere in the early morning darkness.

Moments later, the second man stepped down from the cab, his hands in the air. The face was unfamiliar. He was calm, "so calm it was scary, and very confident," said one policeman.

"I'm Allan Legere."

It was 6:15 A.M., Friday, November 24. The long chase was finally over.

Legere couldn't help but see some numerological significance in it all. He'd been arrested for the Glendenning murder on the twenty-fourth. His divorce from his first wife had occurred on the twenty-fourth. Now the number twenty-four had brought him bad luck again.

Scanners and phones quickly spread the news of his capture.

Crown prosecutor Fred Ferguson was sleeping at the Wharf Inn in Newcastle, just a few hundred feet from the home of the murdered Daughney sisters and about half a mile from the rectory of Father Smith. Ferguson's wife and children were away with relatives, and the security around him was gone. The call on his cellular phone came shortly after Legere's capture.

Half a mile away, RCMP Const. Kevin Mole was running down the hall of the Journey's End motel, his cellular phone to his ear, his jacket half-on.

Mole was one of those who had helped Mary Glendenning during the many months she had recuperated in hospital, talking to her, holding her hand. He'd done the same for Nina Flam when she was recovering from her burns and injuries three years later. Most of his fellow officers considered him one of the best, the most compassionate among them.

"Get up! Get up!" he yelled at Ferguson. "If you don't, you're going to miss the biggest story in the eastern half of North America."

Ferguson knew then that they'd captured Legere. "Where?" he asked, pulling on his pants.

"South Nelson," said Mole.

"Is he alive?"

"You bet."

Ferguson arrived at the RCMP station around seven o'clock. It was still dark. As he jumped out of his car he was met by MacLean of the *Miramichi Leader*. They grabbed each other in a bear hug, pounding each other on the back.

"You don't know how I feel," Ferguson said before rushing into the building. It had been an especially difficult time for him. An RCMP officer had stayed in his home, guarding the prosecutor, his wife, and little boy and girl from possible attack. At one time, an Emergency Response Team member stood guard over the Ferguson house at night, hiding in the top of a lighthouse on the property. When his daughter asked Ferguson what the man was doing in the lighthouse, he said he was taking pictures of the nearly full moon. He must be getting good pictures, she replied.

Ron, the juror from the Glendenning case, received a call from his brother just minutes after the capture. He dressed and drove straight to the RCMP detachment, arriving in time to hear the police helicopter land.

"There was a lot of traffic around, so I didn't stop. I came home and sat around for half an hour and listened to the radio. I went back again and it was still about the same thing going on. But I knew they had him then. It was just like a weight taken off you. It just felt so good. It felt like we weren't being threatened no more."

Billy Matchett hadn't slept again that night. He listened on his scanner to the news of the capture. Matchett thought of going out to South Nelson just to see for himself. He changed his mind and called three or four friends he thought should know.

Premier Frank McKenna got the call almost immediately. He was overjoyed and relieved. "I always believed the RCMP would get him," he later said.

At radio station CFAN, in Newcastle, a woman from Saint John phoned just moments after she had contacted her elderly mother, who lived on the Miramichi. Her mother, suffering from insomnia since the killing of Annie Flam, was able to doze off only fitfully until the sun came up. But no longer. "Mom," the daughter said, "wake up so you can sleep."

At the RCMP detachment, police slapped and hugged each other. They'd worked hard, more than anyone except their families and other officers would ever know.

As if on cue, the snowstorm ended before dawn. The sun shone brightly. People who had once refused to talk to reporters, magically appeared to talk before cameras and microphones.

At a quarter to nine, the bells of St. Michael's basilica in Chatham rang out in celebration. Normally they're rung only for weddings and weekend masses, but the pastor said it was time for rejoicing and thanking God.

"Christmas has come early," someone said.

That afternoon, the RCMP and the local police conducted a news conference at the Newcastle town hall to outline details of the capture. They held it in the main auditorium, to accommodate the crush of reporters. The news release they passed out gave a blow-by-blow account of Legere's capture.

The more than twenty reporters and cameramen were as excited as the police. For many, the story had been the exclusive focus of their lives for the past several months. Newcastle had been their home away from home.

RCMP Supt. Al Rivard said that he wasn't surprised Legere gave up without a fight. "There are certain aspects of Allan Legere that would lead me to believe that he would give up. I always considered him to be somewhat of a coward because of the victims we are alleging he is a suspect in." The syntax was all wrong, but it didn't matter. That was the clip everyone would use.

Cars jammed both sides of the Chaplin Island Road in front of the detachment where Legere was being questioned. Everyone wanted a look at the man who had haunted their waking and sleeping lives for seven months.

Police spoke with him for fourteen hours. Or rather they listened, because he apparently did not stop talking. When he rambled into a discourse on religion, one officer who thought he knew Legere well said to himself, "This isn't Allan."

Rivard came out to speak with reporters that night. He had a photograph of Legere in captivity and the sketch of the accomplice. They were, he told them, one and the same man. Dan Allen had been right.

Legere was supposed to have been taken to the Renous prison at seven o'clock, but it wasn't until just before ten that the metal door at the rear of the detachment slid up. A dozen members of the ERT squad had their rifles at the ready. They weren't taking a chance some crazy would take a shot at their prisoner. Two of them walked on each side of the handcuffed Legere who was wearing green prison fatigues, rubber boots, and sunglasses. There were leg irons around his ankles.

Cameras whirred and lightbulbs flashed.

"Coward," someone shouted.

"Allan Legere," a reporter called, "what do you have to say to the people of the Miramichi?"

"Fuck you," was the response as Legere was placed in an RCMP cruiser. It's not clear whether his answer was meant for the reporter or for Miramichiers.

The car drove into the night, taking Allan Legere back to segregated confinement at Renous.

NINETEEN

Centre-stage

RECAPTURED, Legere quickly reverted to form.

In a nine-page handwritten letter to the Saint John *Telegraph Journal* dated December 1, 1989, the many sides of Allan Legere surfaced. He mocked police and delighted in recounting the details of his final hours of freedom. He denied yet again killing John Glendenning, while admitting that he had lied long and hard when he testified at the 1987 trial. Time and again he returned to the same theme: he was never given a fair shake, never given a break. Here are some excerpts from the letter.

> I've been following most all newspaper, TV, CBC etc. reports since my May "departure". . . .
>
> I've noticed that RCMP [Supt. Al] Rivard calls me a chicken, etc. but do tell me, if I am so chicken and dumb, why couldn't over 100 of Canada's finest, with dogs, and swat teams find little ol' moi? Hmm? It is obvious that in one instance they'd tell the media that I have lots of help and once I'm jailed, I'm suddenly alone? eh? I'm sorry I made them look dumb!

All summer long the swat team rambled through the bush, but as soon as darkness fell, zoom! They all headed for town or home. How come? RCMP [Sgt. Ernie] Munden tells the public around June-July 1st, to go ahead and live as before, since I've no doubt left the area. Yet the RCMP and the Chatham Cops (for sure) *know* I was still around. The Chatham Cops chased a fellow around July 16 and took his discarded beer, so I'm told.

Masterwoodsman? Was that title donated to ease public pressure from their inability to catch me? I only went to the forest to pick berries with my son and daughter in the 1970's or as late as 1986 for a picnic with my gal pal. Now, I'd call myself a 'survivor' and I do know the terrain and forests areas. Honestly, I sincerely believe all those french fellows on the swat team and Newcastle force do watch too much TV and too preoccupied with fancy rifles and the 'cool' look, when all it would take is one good sweep of the forest. At any given time, I was no further than a shout away. Paperback heroes! Flying in a helicopter and sitting in their cruisers.

The newspaper said – 'checkmate!!' I will dispute that by simply saying I forfeited the game!!! I had *control* of the 'board' and captured a 'queen' (female RCMP), a 'Rookie' (cab driver) and a Knight (Mac truck driver). Alas, since the winter arrived one month early, it ruined my strategy just as the Germans lost out in Moscow to old man winter. Plus, I had to practically drive in their (RCMP) back yard before they caught the play (slow movers). Ask the 'truckdriver' because I said to him – 'Where are the roadblocks? By now the other two who eluded me turned up the heat!' I told the truckdriver if he came to a road block to stop and I'd give up. *Period.* I told him to stop the truck for the cops but he bailed out regardless. Nervous I guess! I told the three involved that no harm would come to them. In fact, I told them to charge the media for interviews. The RCMP only reveal the negative reports, for their credit (desperate characters). . . .

No, I never tried to 'date' those dead girls years back and no, I never had dealings with the dead priest. In fact, I attended Church regularly until about 1964 when I went to Confession before Rev Monroe (now deceased) and he told me not to return to Church if I kept sleeping with my girlfriend and later wife. So I stayed away. I don't think he knew how to properly tell me. . . .

By the way, I always got along with the Miramichi girls! I can still recall 88 or so names. One is a 'lawyer,' one is a 'teller' and secretaries and housewifes, etc. (Love'em all). . . .

Now, the 1986 June 21 Glendenning killing:

As the evidence (re transcripts) goes, two sets of foot prints go across to the house. One set goes through the muddy ditch 1/4 miles up wind where the car is parked. I walked through the mud to follow the 2 assholes because although we all thought nobody was home, I wasn't sure if they could even find a safe in an empty house. . . .

As I arrived, I could hear the door being booted and sure enough there was Scott Curtis and Todd Matchett (co-accused) struggling with Mr. and Mrs. Glendenning. Since nobody was supposed to be home, I had no gloves, no mask, so I didn't enture too close, although I did stop Curtis from continuously kicking the old fellow after he ran from the house to the highway. . . .

After I tried the safe dial, both punks started beating on them again, so I stopped it and said – 'Just take the safe as they won't tell you zip.' I went for the car and when I returned, Curtis said he wasn't sure if the old guy was breathing. No wonder, as I went upstairs I seen that Curtis had tied a rag over the victims facial area very tight. I slid it over and I could hear him breath. When they drove me to my girlfriends (Christine Searle) apartment in Chatham I told the fellows that I'd call the ambulance. Curtis said if I did that, they'd get caught on route to Saint John. So I didn't. . . .

In my trial, *No evidence* ever surfaced, even by Mrs. Glendenning, to show I *ever* harmed either person!! She, in fact, testified it was the 2 younger lads who beat her and her husband. . . .

"Yet the N.B. Appeal Court wouldn't give me a retrial (*prejudice*) and the S.C.O.C. [Supreme Court of Canada] dragged its feet and I believe *were influenced* by N.B. Appeal court to not give *this* person a new trial! "That's why I took off! . . ."

At my trial, Jan 6/87, *not one* of the jurors were asked whether they were prejudiced against me and I knew over half of them. And I have *never* (I know where they are but none were bothered) threatened *any* juror. I have copies of my Oct/88 registered letters to them and basically I say – 'Why didn't you people stand up and tell the judge that you knew of my terrible notorious reputation?' . . .

The people who were scared were scared because of a guilty conscience, including local newspapers who always condemn me, or Pros. [Fred] Ferguson whom I despise for what he did. And [RCMP] Sgt. Mason Johnston got a

Bouctouche Detachment for getting me convicted by saying I told him I was at crime scene, which I didn't say! No statement, no tape, yet old Judge [Paul] Godin, the cops pal, let it be evidence. (all are 'trough feeders,' you know.)

Now I see Mason Johnston told the Miramichi Papers last week that I hugged him! *What lies!* I was handcuffed legs (and not given a lawyer) and hands behind my back, stripped naked (and earlier after I gave up, kicked in face by frog RCMP 'Bolduc') (Lots of Legere around). I *never* hugged Johnston but did ask him to tell the french RCMP to uncuff me. Period. The only place I'd hug Johnston is over the grand canyon with an anvil....

I do know that during my abscence, the RCMP *did* enter my cell at Renous and I noticed that all along they'd accuse me but as the pressure grew from no arrest, I now believe they add my cell 'hair' (scalp, etc) amongst anything found in any crime scenes. You know – 'Oh, look what I found!' How else could they suddenly tell the public it must be me? The dogs!...

[In 1979] I was drunk, a guy hit me and Cst. Donny Butler of Chatham, moonlighting as a bouncer, broke my jaw with a pool cue. I got from Aug 1979 to March 1981 in jail for threats, all in Moncton Detention Center! Nobody else charged or hurt. In 1982 Cst. Mahar of Moncton shot me in the back, not arrested nor armed. I was only a *suspect* in an overnight Break & Entry....

Everybody who has wronged me in *any way* always pays the price, for its the law of the universe. Cst. Butler who broke my jaw has since had severe back problems and a crippled child. Cst Mahar is paying his dues. Chief Allen has his 'personal' problems, Chief [Greg] Cohoon [of the

Moncton police department] has arthritic problems and I swear, all who have judged will be judged by their own measures.

Me pay for anything? I've been paying all my life. Like Lee Hazlewood and Nancy Sinatra once sang in the 60's – I've been down so long, it looks like up to me.

The Bible. People don't understand the Bible. The people who mind their business and do their thing are honest and non-judging, don't have to know it. Priest are sexually abusing boys for years as in Mt. Cashel, Nfld. (I wonder where else). Samson killed 100's of bastards of Romans, etc. and is a Biblical hero. St. Pat persecuted Christians and looted churches, etc. Now people pray to his little statues. Moses murdered a soldier and yet was seen fit by God to lead the Israelites for 40 years. The friends of Christ were whores and thieves. People pray to statues of Christ, etc. yet nobody knows what they looked like. Remember, Christ will not come back as a lamb, *but a lion!* And Lucifer was God's chief angel before the fall. Lucifer was very powerful since nobody believes in him anymore. Only when they are scared do they pray. Lucifer *cannot* do anything to anybody except with God's permission of course. The end times? I sincerely believe so. Probably by the year 2000. Only God knows for sure. 'Nuff said!' . . .

I left my wife in 1977 because (mainly) of RCMP harrassment. They had me doing murders, etc. that I *never* committed! My boy was at school and kids were talking. I blamed myself for a lot of it, but I hate the local and RCMP coppers. They were worse than me, because they were *using* the law as terrorist. . . .

At my Dec. 1986 change of venue in Moncton Court, Chief Allen and Pros. Ferguson told 'Judge Godin' that I'd get a '*fair trial*' in Newcastle. (Sure, right where Pros. Ferguson has been trying to jail me for 15 years and prior to my being charged in 1986 for Murder, people (500) yelled for my hanging!!! FAIR trial my ass! Like a cop said, we give you a fair trial Al, then hang you.). . . .

Bottom line is, all I wanted was a fair trial so I could get a lesser sentence for the '86 crime. Like 10 or 12 years just for being there. Then get out and at my age settle down for good and possibly contribute to society by counselling young fellows on the wrong path. But no, they wouldn't do dick for me. So if you take my life, I'll fight!

To this date, I've never spent a penny of the 1986 safe money. Christine Searle got 900.00 for sure. And when I got out, the rest of it was gone. I told the RCMP to their face (last week) that *they* stole it and kept it rather than give it back. *Only* a dog, a police dog, could have found it (only I know) where and it *was found on June 24, 1986* when I got arrested and the cops searched the area! (That's why I couldn't leave the country this time).

All in all, I was as brief as possible. If a book ever comes about, I'll detail it from A to Z and until that time, I'll say good day and when it comes to Chess and the game of life, RCMP 'boys', you'll have to get up awful early in the A.M.!

Of course, I'd probably have to knock on your door and ask to be arrested 'like this time' – eh Rivard? Parlez vous des buckwheat?

The letter, excerpts of which ran in newspapers across Canada, put Legere back where he has always lived to be – centre-stage. But at least he was securely behind bars this time. Or so it was hoped.

Today no one at the Atlantic Institution talks to

Legere. Certainly not the prisoners – some, in fact, say they would like to kill the "star" inmate – and certainly not the guards. Legere embarrassed security staff by escaping in May 1989. He showed that they had been played for fools.

Alone in his cell, Allan Legere now is the ultimate loner in a society of losers.

EPILOGUE

Footsteps in the Dark

This story is, of course, incomplete.

Murder charges were expected to be laid against Allan Legere sometime shortly after this book was written. It promises to be a long legal fight, with attempts to have the trial moved out of the Miramichi and gut-wrenching testimony about what happened during the last hours of the lives of Annie Flam, Donna and Linda Daughney, and Father James Smith. If the John Glendenning murder case is any measure, the legal battles could continue for years.

The Miramichi may never be the same. While people are eager to put this grisly story behind them, they're also bracing for the expected trials. Most just want to forget. Many disliked the decision to write a book about the seven months of fear and pain they went through. The Miramichi is like a big family. You don't wash your dirty linen in public. The murders painted the area as some sort of breeding ground for killers. That stung. The people want the microscope to go looking elsewhere.

They'll get what they want, eventually. People will forget, the cameras and reporters will move on to fresher stories. But it won't be so simple for the people of the Miramichi. Some hope to use what has happened as a springboard to get the community more involved in fighting crime, to make people realize that crime is not just a police problem. A committee of community leaders and police has been set up to try to get people more involved. The RCMP seem determined to regain their position of trust and respect in the Miramichi, something they lost in the past few years when they came to be seen as aloof and uncaring.

Others, perhaps many others, struggle to come to terms with what this episode has done to them personally. For many, the terror created during the months of murder forced them to look into a place better forgotten – the abyss of fear where death is so real you can feel it breathing on you.

On December 10, barely two weeks after Legere was caught, Sara Lynch, sixty-four, and her nineteen-year-old daughter Rhonda were found murdered in their Newcastle home, just around the corner from Morrissy Doran's house. They had been asphyxiated. Later that same day, a seventeen-year-old male surrendered to police. He has since been charged with the double murder.

Betty and Tom of Newcastle recall that Sunday vividly. "When we first heard that, we were just ready to eat," Betty said. "Our sister and brother from Halifax were here and Sam [a relative in Saint John] called. We couldn't believe it at first. We knew them well. I thought Sam must have got it wrong. We looked at each other and said, 'It's started again.' We went to church that night and somebody told us they got a fellow and that was kind of a relief."

Life can never be as it was for Betty and Tom. The pipe wrench still rests next to the bed. It's the same for Ron the juror. Nearly a month after Legere's capture, his rifle is still propped next to his bed, still loaded. "I guess it just takes a while to sink in that he's caught. I'll take it out some of these days. I'll leave the gun there, but I'll take the bullets out of it."

The Miramichi, one man told a reporter, will be hearing footsteps in the dark for a long time.

More Great Titles from M&S Paperbacks...

THE REGIMENT
by Farley Mowat
Heroism and horror during the Italian campaign of WWII. "Few novels can match this book for sheer excitement and suspense." - *London Free Press*
0-7710-6694-5 $8.95 Includes 17 pages of maps

CHARLES
A Biography
by Anthony Holden
"A well-written, reflective analysis of a complex man, bewildered by a life he doesn't want." - *Ottawa Citizen*
0-7710-4194-2 $6.95 Includes 32 pages of photos

LADYBUG, LADYBUG...
by W.O. Mitchell
"Funny, frightening and enlightening, a treat for Mitchell fans." - *Halifax Daily News*
0-7710-6076-9 $5.95

WELCOME TO FLANDERS FIELDS
by Daniel G. Dancocks
A spellbinding account of the men and events in the battle that became a benchmark of Canadian history.
0-7710-2546-7 $5.95 Includes 16 pages of photos

ABOVE TOP SECRET
The Worldwide UFO Cover-up
by Timothy Good
The most comprehensive and authoritative book on UFOs ever written.
0-7710-3364-8 $7.95

More Great Titles from M&S Paperbacks...

PLATINUM BLUES
by William Deverell
Step behind the scenes of the gritty, no-holds-barred world of rock music in this tension-packed new thriller from the author of Needles.
0-7710-2662-5 $5.95

NIGHTS BELOW STATION STREET
by David Adams Richards
"A voice to be reckoned with." - *Globe and Mail*
A powerful tale of family conflict, vividly set in New Brunswick. Winner of the Governor General's award for fiction.
0-7710-7461-1 $5.95

NOW BACK TO YOU DICK
by Dick Irvin
"He writes, he scores!" - *Montreal Gazette*
The famous broadcaster gives an insider's view of some of hockey's most thrilling moments.
0-7710-4354-6 $5.95 Includes 32 pages of photos

ROBINSON FOR THE DEFENCE
by Larry Robinson with Chrys Goyens
A first-person look at the NHL by professional hockey's best defenceman.
0-7710-7551-0 $5.95 Includes 16 pages of photos

THE CANADIAN ESTABLISHMENT, Vol. 1
by Peter C. Newman
"An astonishing book...a fascinating encyclopedia...a Canadian who's who." - *Toronto Star*
0-7710-6777-1 $7.95

JOURNEY
by James A. Michener
From the master story teller, a terrific tale of five goldseekers' gruelling travels in Canada's north.
0-7710-5866-7 $5.95

Photos: Duane Cummings

RICK MACLEAN, 32, has been editor of the *Miramichi Leader* community newspaper in Newcastle, N.B., since 1984. He has an M.A. in journalism from the University of Western Ontario and is a former member of the Canadian foreign service. This is his second book. His first book was on the life of a Britsh civil servant living in India in the 1800s. He is working with former jockey Ron Turcotte on his autobiography. He is married with one child.

ANDRÉ VENIOT, 39, has been a reporter for 20 years, the last six with CBC TV News in New Brunswick. Veniot is a regular contributor to CBC Radio's "Morningside." Veniot served for two years with CUSO in West Africa. He's married with two children and lives near Moncton.

8 pages of photos!
Exclusive interviews!

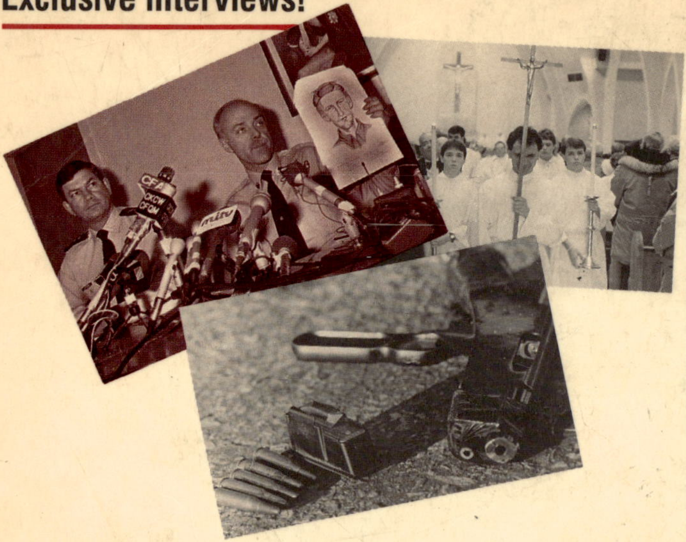

Would the killing never end? As summer gave way to fall in 1989, residents of New Brunswick's picturesque Miramichi River region found themselves hostages of terror. Four people, including a 69-year-old Catholic priest, had been brutally murdered in their homes. Police responded with one of the largest manhunts in Canadian history. People went to bed at night with guns and knives by their side. But still peace would not come...

Written by two veteran New Brunswick journalists, TERROR is the gripping, authoritative story of one province's agony and the efforts made to end it.

Non-Fiction/Crime

M&S

An M&S Paperback Original from
McClelland & Stewart Inc.
The Canadian Publishers

ISBN 0-7710-5592-7